PRAISE FOR

Diana Palmer has published over seventy category romances, as well as historical romances and longer contemporary works. With over forty million copies of her books in print, Diana Palmer is one of North America's most beloved authors. Her accolades include two *Romantic Times* Reviewer's Choice Awards, a Maggie Award, five national Waldenbooks bestseller awards and two national B. Dalton bestseller awards. Diana resides in the north mountains of her home state of Georgia with her husband, James, and their son, Blayne Edward.

DIANA PALMER

To Love and Cherish

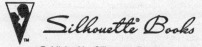

Silhouette® Books

Published by Silhouette Books

America's Publisher of Contemporary Romance

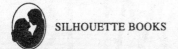 SILHOUETTE BOOKS

ISBN 0-373-51209-0

TO LOVE AND CHERISH

First published in North America as a MacFadden Romance by Kim Publishing Corporation.

Copyright © 1979 by Diana Palmer.

One

Shelby Kane packed her suitcase with a feeling of impending doom. A week on a ranch the size of Skylance would have delighted most girls, but she couldn't feel any enthusiasm for another confrontation with Kingston Brannt. The last one had caused her to leave the Texas ranch in tears in the middle of the night.

She wished she'd never agreed to

go to Branntville with Danny for a week's vacation. It had been one of those spur-of-the-moment decisions. They were enjoying a night at a new San Antonio disco bar when Danny grinned at her and said, "Come home with me on your vacation. Mom and Dad would be delighted. You know how they dote on you."

That much was true. Kate and Jim Brannt had welcomed Shelby the first time she set foot on Skylance, and the affection they had for her had grown over the years. It was King who made such infrequent visits an ordeal. She shivered at just the memory of that hard, dark face with its jutting brow and piercing dark eyes. He was as hard as the country he ranched, as tough and unyielding as saddle leather. And he hated "city ladies." If Shelby had been a working girl, or somebody's homely cousin, he might have been kinder. But she had an elfin face and brown velvet eyes and short, straight hair the color of black diamonds, and she earned her living as a model. Not that she needed to work. Her mother was a famous actress, internationally known. Shelby could have had anything she wanted if she'd been less proud. A little flattery and pleading would have gotten her anything she wanted from Maria Kane. But what Shelby wanted most was independence. She wanted to make her own way, and she'd done it, to her mother's chagrin. But King didn't know how hard Shelby had to fight to gain her independence, and he didn't care. As far as he was concerned, Shelby was purely decorative; unfit for ranch life, for anything but the life of a spoiled society brat.

The door to her bedroom burst open suddenly, startling her, and her roommate Edie Jackson bounced in like a red-headed ball of lightning.

"You're not going back to Sky-lance again!" she exclaimed.

"You've seen Danny, I suppose," Shelby sighed.

"Well, I do work for him," Edie reminded her with a smile. "Anyway, is it true?"

"Just for my vacation," Shelby admitted, as she stuffed another pair of tailored jeans into her suitcase. "If you can call five days a vacation, and I was really lucky to get that many. I'm modeling Jomar's fall collection show in two weeks; just one of many lucky girls," she teased.

"Of which you're tops, and they know it," Edie said kindly. "Is King going to be at the ranch?"

Shelby shuddered. "I don't know."

Edie looked worried. She plopped down on the scarlet bedspread beside the suitcase with a frown. "Oh, Shelby, don't go back," she pleaded.

"Not after what that man did to you last time. He'll just make it unbearable for you."

"Maybe it will be better this time," Shelby said in her soft, husky voice.

"That's what you said last time," her friend reminded her. "And it wasn't. There's something about you that makes a madman of Kingston Brannt. Danny said as much himself last time. He thinks it's that you remind King of a girl who threw him over years ago."

"I'll be okay," Shelby said with a smile, mentally hoping she was right. She closed the suitcase and locked it.

"Will you do something for me?" Edie asked. "If it gets too rough, will you call me this time instead of leaving the house in the middle of the night and walking the two miles to town to catch a bus? Will you please pick up the phone and call me?"

The memory of that midnight walk turned Shelby's high-cheekboned face a delicate pink. King had gone crazy, Danny told her later, when he discovered her room empty. Which was nothing to the explosion that was still echoing in her mind when he found out what she'd done. He'd called her at work, frightening one of the other models to death when she answered the phone, and spent five minutes raking her over the coals for leaving Skylance without telling anyone. What if you'd been picked up by some drunk? he'd raged at her. She meant to tell him that even that would have been preferable to another day in his home putting up with his temper and his intolerance and his insults. But she'd only listened. And then gently, quietly, she'd put the receiver down with King's voice still roaring from the other end of the line. He hadn't called back, and she hadn't seen him since. That was six months ago. And now she was walking right back into the tiger's lair again, voluntarily. She sighed. Maybe insanity did run in her family after all.

"Are you going to marry Danny?" Edie probed gently.

"No," Shelby said with a smile. "I'm terribly fond of him, and we have lots of fun together, but I feel toward him more like a sister would, and I think he knows it. Marriage needs to be more than simple affection."

Edie sighed. "You could do worse than an up and coming young lawyer with a filthy rich family."

"I suppose. But that's not what I want. I'm not a social animal," she added, cringing a little when she remembered her childhood. It seemed to consist of one endless round of cocktail parties and laughter and drunk men and "uncles" who slept in. Her mother had married four times already, and was supposedly about to divorce Brad—her latest—for someone else. Shelby felt sorry for Brad. He was the best of the lot, and he genuinely loved Maria Kane. But whatever Maria felt, her only child wasn't privileged to know. Maria only managed a card every Christmas, or some indifferent kind of expensive gift on Shelby's birthday. Once in a great while, when she was depressed over some role or another, she'd call to cry on Shelby's shoulder. But she never called out of affection, or out of love. Those emotions weren't part of Maria's repertoire.

"Hear, hear," Edie glowered. "I can't even get you to go with me to a party."

"Especially when you're trying to play matchmaker," Shelby laughed.

"You're the strangest woman I

know,'' the older woman sighed. ''Shelby, you're twenty-one. Isn't it time you hung up those archaic ideas of yours and lived a little?''

''No,'' Shelby said quietly. ''I'm not the swinging type. When and if the right man ever comes along, I want something permanent, not a loose arrangement that depends on nothing but desire to keep it alive. I like children, you know.''

Edie shook her head. ''You just won't get involved with anyone, though. Are you afraid of men?'' she teased.

''Terrified,'' she kidded, but it was no joke. She really was afraid of anything binding. Loving made you vulnerable. She wasn't ever going to be vulnerable.

''You will call me?'' Edie pleaded, and the concern was in her whole look.

Shelby touched her friend's arm lightly. "I will. Take care."

"I always do. You take care, my friend," Edie told her. "Kingston Brannt eats little girls for breakfast."

"I'll give him heartburn," Shelby laughed.

Edie had already gone back to the office when Danny Brannt came by to pick Shelby up. He grinned at her as she opened the door, taking in the amber slacks and matching loose knit top that complimented her olive complexion and her dark hair and eyes.

"Pretty as a picture," he commented. "Why don't you go into modeling for a living?"

"I'm too fat," she said, tongue-in-cheek, and they both laughed.

Danny Brannt had a sense of humor, something Shelby couldn't credit King with. King almost never smiled. He took life seriously, somberly, and his was wrapped up in cattle and oil. Danny never stopped smiling, and while he enjoyed the legal profession, he never took it, or life, too seriously. Like Shelby, he didn't have to work. His father and King would have given him any job he wanted in the family's mammoth holdings. But Danny was young and independent and he liked law. He did a lot of free counseling, working in a legal aid society and he was a crusader for equal rights. Shelby admired that facet of his personality. She believed in causes, too, and she'd been known to march in rallies if she believed strongly enough. Gentle she might be, but she had enough spirit to stand up and be counted.

There were physical dissimilarities between Danny and his older brother, too. Danny was shorter, stockier, and six years younger than King. His hair was a light brown, his eyes green like his mother's. He didn't have King's dark complexion and features. It was like the difference between night and day.

"What are you thinking about so hard?" Danny asked, lifting her suitcase while she turned out the lights in the apartment and closed and locked the door behind them.

"How different you are from King," she said quietly.

The grin faded. He put her in the sporty green Jaguar and got in beside her. "I'm sorry you two don't get along," he said gently. "But King's going to be away on business. You won't see him."

She touched his sleeve, surprising a strange look in his eyes. "Danny, don't let me cause friction between you and your brother."

"You won't," he replied. He smiled. "King and I are a team, Shelby. I'd do anything for him, and it's mutual. But he has this…thing about city women. I'm sorry he's taking past hurts out on you. I never thought he'd be like that.''

He didn't know the half, she thought miserably; and she was glad she'd never told him the truth about that night she left the ranch. She turned in the seat to face him as the sports car ate up the miles out of San Antonio, heading toward Branntville. ''He doesn't seem the kind of man to let anyone hurt him,'' she probed gently.

''A woman can get next to the hardest heart, didn't you know?'' he laughed. ''King's not invincible, and he wasn't immune to Sandy. She left him for an insurance salesman. I think that hurt most of all; that the guy wasn't even rich.''

''Was it a long time ago?''

''Five years or more. King was always hard, but that made him like

steel. Even now, he doesn't date anyone regularly, except Janice Edson,
and he's not serious about her. It's a
form of self-protection, I imagine,
that he won't commit himself again.
He doesn't want to let anyone get
close.''

She sighed. ''I know how that
feels. But I wish he wouldn't take it
out on me,'' she said with a smile.
''He's rough on my nerves.''

''Fight back, Shelby,'' he advised
gently. ''He respects spirit; he can't
take it when people knuckle under. It
makes him lose his temper.''

''I'm not that much of a fighter. I
never have been.''

''No,'' he agreed. ''You're a gentle little fawn, and that's probably the
whole trouble. Men want to protect
you, little one. Even men like King.
That must rankle like hell, as much
as he despises women.''

''I don't understand.''

"I know. But I do," he chuckled.

"Danny?" she puzzled.

"Let's tell the folks we're getting married," he said unexpectedly.

Her eyes dilated wildly. "What?" she burst out.

"Oh, not for real," he said comfortingly. "For a lark. If King thinks you're going to be one of the family, he'll stop grinding his heel into you. Think of it as armour, Shelby," he told her. "Protection."

"I'm not sure... My gosh, Danny, what would your parents think?"

"That I was finally showing some intelligence," he replied. "They stay on me all the time about getting married. They know King isn't going to, and they're getting older every day. They want grandchildren," he said, almost strangling on the word.

"Oh, I begin to see the light," she said, nodding. "You're the one who needs protection."

"Both of us," he amended. He looked absolutely hunted. "I want to get married someday. But I'm only twenty-six. I've just begun to live. I don't want to tie myself down yet!"

"No, think of the hearts you'd break!" she teased.

"Thank God yours isn't one of them," he said, glancing at her solemnly. "That's why I suggested the pretence. You're the sister I never had, and that's God's own truth. There's never been anything emotional with us, and there won't be. But King could tear you up pretty bad, and I'm getting hell from all sides about my life style. Let's help each other out."

She pursed her lips. "It might be fun, at that. But I don't have a ring."

"I thought we might have to do something about that." He handed her a jeweler's box. "Open it. Edie helped me pick it out just before I left the office today.''

''Edie?''

He chuckled. ''She'd do anything she thought would protect you from King,'' he admitted. ''She doesn't have a high opinion of my brother.''

Shelby didn't, either, but she wasn't going to hurt Danny's feelings by agreeing with Edie. She opened the box and took out a small diamond ring.

''Danny, this is too...'' she began.

''Never mind, just put it on,'' he replied.

She slid the yellow gold band with its fiery stone onto the third finger of her left hand and stared at it. ''But Danny...''

''When our 'engagement' is over,'' he said soothingly, ''I know a lovely lady who wears a ring just that size that I intend to give it to one day. Fair enough?''

She sat back, shaking her head. "I just don't understand."

"You will," he said with a smug grin. "You will."

Skylance was a throwback to trail-driving days in Texas. Located on the old Chisolm cattle trail, it was in the heart of cattle country, a massive working ranch in the center of a wealth of dude ranches that catered to Eastern tourists who wanted a look at the "real" West without any of the discomforts of "roughing it."

The ranch stretched for thousands of miles, and was rich in oil as well as cattle. Shelby sighed, her eyes drinking in the lush green fields that stretched over the softly sloping landscape where herds of Santa Gertrudis grazed, their distinctive red coats readily visible in the bright sunlight. Those fields which, in springtime, were covered with bluebells and brown-eyed herds of Texas longhorns in the old days when they were driven to market over the famous Chisolm Trail to northern and western markets. Unlike West Texas, where scrub brush and mesquite and cacti and desert stretched for miles toward the Mexican border, this part of Texas was lush and green and fertile. Huge pecan trees, the state tree, lay in groves along the road they traveled, shaded houses far off the highway. Of course, there was mesquite around here, too, with its infinite roots trying to take over the pastures. It was as pesky to the rancher as morning glories were to a Georgia gardener.

"Missing the city?" Danny teased.

"Oh, terribly," she returned laughingly. Her eyes closed and she sighed. "I'd love to live here," she murmured. "Just endless fields and horses to ride and peace and quiet. I wouldn't even mind seeing a camera again."

"Peace and quiet you won't find this particular weekend," he warned her. "There's a fiesta. And a barbecue. Even a river race." He glanced at her. "And a square dance."

Her big, dark eyes lit up. "I'd love the square dance if I can find a partner."

"Don't look at me," he said in mock terror. "You know how fumble-footed I am." He glanced at her strangely. "King knows the steps."

She turned her oval face toward the car's window and the smile left her lips.

"Sorry," he said sheepishly.

"It's all right."

"I wish the two of you got along better."

"It doesn't matter. Anyway," she recalled with a smile, "he won't be there."

Danny looked guilty. "Uh, Shelby, there's just one thing I forgot to mention...."

Before he could finish the sentence, there was a roar behind them and the sound of a horn. Danny glanced into the rear view mirror and a wild, daredevil light came into his green eyes.

"Looks like a race," he murmured, and Shelby recognized the private road that led to Skylance as Danny jerked the steering wheel and turned the small sports car off the main road onto the ranch road.

Danny's hand worked the gearshift feverishly, the force of speed throwing Shelby back against the cushy leather seat. The roar behind them got louder and the low-slung black Porsche came alongside, hesitated, then shot forward like a black bullet giving an insolent long honk as it easily outdistanced the little Jaguar and vanished around a curve into the grove of towering oak and pecan trees.

Shelby had recognized the other car, and her accusing dark eyes met Danny's as he pulled up in front of the 19th century Victorian house that was the Brannt homeplace.

"Sorry," Danny said genuinely. "But I knew you wouldn't come with me if I leveled with you, and I needed you here with me. I'll tell you the real reason later."

"What makes you think I'll be speaking to you later?" she asked half-amusedly as she watched Kingston Brannt emerge with cat-like grace from the black Porsche.

Two

He was as intimidating as ever. Tall, lean, whipcord muscled, and as elegant as any male model in the brown slacks and cream colored sports shirt he was wearing. He approached the car lighting a cigarette, but his fingers froze on the lighter as he looked into the Jag and spotted Shelby sitting next to his brother. His face went harder than stone, but his eyes even at the distance began to catch fire. Shelby stiffened instinctively and fought down an urge to get out of the car and run. She was more afraid of King than she'd ever been of any human being. She'd never understood why, but the fear was real and definite. Especially after her last visit here.

"Hey, calm down," Danny said gently, noticing the rigid set of her slender body, the wide-eyed panic in her flushed face.

King finished lighting his cigarette and pocketed the lighter with ill-concealed violence. He watched Danny get out of the car and greeted him warmly, but his eyes were still on Shelby, never wandering even when Danny came around to help her out of the little car.

She moved away from the door stiffly, hanging onto Danny's hand as if salvation depended on it.

"Hello, Shelby," King said quietly.

She couldn't meet those smouldering dark eyes. Her gaze went no higher than his firm, hard mouth.

"Hello, King," she replied.

"We weren't expecting you," he persisted, with a sharp glance at Danny.

"Mom and Dad were," Danny corrected with a smile. "We came down to tell them about our engagement."

King's eyes seemed to explode at the statement. "You and Shelby?" he asked curtly, as if the idea was ridiculous.

"Me and Shelby," Danny nodded. "Well, aren't you going to congratulate us?"

The older man took a long draw from his cigarette, studying Shelby's flushed face. "Where do you plan on living? San Antonio? I can't see

Shelby settling for life on a ranch when she's so used to night life," he bit off.

Shelby bit her lip and turned her face into Danny's shoulder, hating her own weakness, the tears that threatened. Danny's hand contracted on her arm.

"Do you have to attack her before she gets her feet on the ground good?" Danny challenged hotly.

"I'm not attacking her," King said mildly. "I just can't see her fitting in here," he added darkly.

Danny put his arm around Shelby's thin shoulders. "Let's go tell the folks, honey," he said gently. "Come on."

She pressed close against Danny's side, not looking at King as they walked past him.

"Shelby..." King began.

She kept her eyes lowered. "I'll only be here for the week, King," she said in a voice that was little more than a whisper. "I won't get in your way."

"Oh, hell!" King growled. He turned on his heel and stalked away toward the ranch office just down the road from the house.

"Buck up," Danny told her with a brotherly hug and grin. "The worst part's over. It'll be downhill now."

Kate Brannt came into the hall to greet them, hugging her son and then Shelby with a warm affection that made her feel part of the family.

"You look lovely, my dear, but far too thin," Kate teased, shaking her silver head with a smile. "Modeling is causing you to waste away."

Shelby smiled. "At least I don't have to worry about getting fat," she laughed.

"I think she looks fantastic," Danny said. "By the way, Mom, we're getting married."

Kate's face froze, and Shelby saw a curious hesitation, and something like pain, touch the thin patrician features. It wasn't that Kate didn't approve of her, Shelby knew, but something was definitely wrong.

The older woman recovered quickly, placing an affectionate arm around Shelby to draw her into the living room with its brown and beige decor. The air-conditioning felt delicious after the taste of southern Texas heat that was unusual for this time of the year.

"I'm delighted that we can finally get you into the family," Kate said, and there was genuine feeling in her voice. "It just comes as a bit of a shock. You and Danny always seemed more like brother and sister to me."

Danny chuckled and sent a knowing wink at Shelby. "Did we, now?" he asked, tongue-in-cheek.

Kate sat down on the dark brown brocade sofa, motioning Shelby to a seat beside her.

"Have you told Kingston?" Kate asked hesitantly.

So that was it, Shelby thought, she was worried about how her eldest son was going to react to the engagement. The whole family must know about his prejudice....

"We told him," Danny said with a heavy sigh. He plopped down in an armchair across from the sofa.

"And?" his mother probed gently.

Danny shrugged. "He made some sarcastic remark about Shelby not adapting to ranch life, and when she promised to keep out of his way while she was here, he threw out a cuss word and stomped off into the sunset."

Kate's eyes closed briefly. "I see."

"I wish I did," Shelby said. "I don't understand him."

"I do," the older woman said quietly. "I only wish I could help." The pained look left her face and she smiled. "Enough about that. Tell me all the news. It's been weeks since I've been in San Antonio!"

Shelby was just finishing an anecdote about her latest modeling assignment when Jim Brannt came in, his silver hair gleaming in the light, his dark eyes smiling as they lit on Shelby and his son.

"Well, well, I hear champagne's in order," he said with a grin. "King just told me."

"Speaking of old grumpy," Danny grinned, "where'd he go?"

"To help Handy fix a fence."

Danny blinked. "In his street clothes?"

Jim shook his thick thatch of silver

hair out of his eyes. "Seemed kind of strange to me, too," he said.

"I made him lose his temper," Shelby said in her soft voice. "As usual, I'm afraid," she added wryly. "I rub him the wrong way."

"Nothing unusual," Jim chuckled deeply. "Everything's been rubbing him wrong for months. I guess it's his age—he's restless. I know how he feels, too; when I hit thirty-two, I wanted to throw up my hands, get out of the cattle business, and go fly hot air balloons."

"Have you made arrangements to let the men off tomorrow for the fiesta?" Kate asked her husband.

"All but three, who swore they couldn't care less about chili cook-offs and river races," he laughed. "Older hands, you know. Old Ben Ballew was one of them, and you know how he hates parades and crowds."

"We'll enjoy it, though," Kate said with a smile at her ruggedly attractive husband. She reached out and patted Shelby's hand. "So will Shelby. She's never been here for the fiesta before."

"I'll look forward to it," Shelby said. She smiled, but her heart wasn't in it. She was already wishing she'd never come. King was going to give her hell again, she just knew it.

He didn't come in for supper, and it wasn't until the elder Brannts had gone up to bed, leaving Danny and Shelby alone in the living room, that King finally came back to the house.

He took off his ranch hat and tossed it unerringly onto the rack in the hall. His boots were dusty and his once-immaculate pale yellow shirt had traces of dust and grease on it. King looked unspeakably weary. His face was heavily lined, his step slower and less spirited than usual as he came into the living room. His face was proof of the iron control that was part of him, showing no trace of emotion. His dark eyes were equally unreadable as they flashed from Shelby to Danny as he walked to the bar. He splashed bourbon into a glass and added ice to it before he dropped into a deep leather armchair by the fireplace and lit a cigarette.

"Get the fence fixed?" Danny asked with raised eyebrows.

"Um hum," King murmured. He lifted the cigarette to his chiseled mouth and gazed piercingly at Shelby, who dropped her eyes rather than try to survive that intense scrutiny.

"Lose any cattle through it?" Danny persisted.

"No."

"Did it take long to fix?"

"Yes."

"God, you're talkative tonight!" Danny said, exasperated.

"What would you like me to say," King asked thinly, "Congratulations?" He made the single word sound like an insult.

Before Danny could answer him, the phone rang and seconds later Mrs. Denton, the housekeeper, stuck her head in the door to call Danny.

"It's for you," she told him, smiling at Shelby. "Hello, Miss Kane. I saw your mother in a movie on television just last night. She's such a good actress!"

"Thank you," Shelby said automatically.

"Well, I'll say goodnight." Mrs. Denton turned and ambled away, leaving Danny to close the door behind them on his way to the phone.

King didn't speak, but Shelby felt the heat of his eyes as she sat rigidly on the sofa, her hands gripping each other painfully. She didn't want to be alone with King. The room was suddenly too small and stifled with smouldering emotions.

"Afraid of me, Shelby?" he asked, shattering the silence with the low, cold question.

"No," she said softly.

"Then look at me."

She raised her elfin face slowly, her huge brown eyes meeting his across the distance. His eyes darkened, narrowed. He lifted the cigarette to his lips without releasing her from the penetrating gaze that suddenly, inexplicably made her heart cut cartwheels.

"This engagement is rather sudden, isn't it?" he asked finally in a conversational tone. "You and Danny have known each other for over two years; time enough to spare for getting engaged."

"It...uh, it just...happened like that," she said helplessly.

He studied her in a smouldering silence. "You'll never make him happy," he said. "He needs a sparrow, not a peacock."

She tore her eyes away. "I'm not a peacock."

"Hell," he swore impatiently, "you know you're beautiful, I don't have to tell you. But looks don't matter much in marriage. There are more important things; common interests, caring, commitment. I doubt seriously that you're capable of any of them."

"You don't know me, King," she said quietly.

"Like mother, like daughter," he said harshly. "How many husbands has 'mama' gone through—five, six? All that beauty, and every bit of it's surface. She's like you, butterfly—delicate, ornamental, and utterly useless. You'd take to ranch life as easily as you'd take to shooting white water on the river.''

She felt her face going red at the cold insolence in the remarks. As if he knew anything about her! He'd never taken the time or the trouble to find out what she was really like, avoiding her presence at the ranch for the most part as if she'd been invisible. She bit her lower lip to still its trembling. ''Danny won't live on the ranch,'' she hedged softly.

''Hell, no, he won't, as long as he's got this misguided passion for you!'' he lashed at her, his dark eyes narrow and burning. ''Why don't you just let him get it out of his system?''

She went, if possible, redder. Her whole body trembled as she got to her feet. It was worse than a beating, having to sit and be degraded with those cold insults.

''You'll never marry him,

Shelby,'' he said as she reached for the doorknob. "I promise you. No matter what I have to do to stop it, I will.''

She held onto the doorknob with fingers that went white under the strain.

"Nothing to say, Shelby?'' he growled.

She opened the door and went out of the room, closing it gently behind her.

Danny came out of the den with a worried frown on his smooth face.

"Oh, there you are,'' he said abruptly. He stuck his hands in his pockets. "She's coming tomorrow to go to the festival with us,'' he grumbled. "It was King's idea, I'd stake my life on it. She said he rode over to talk to her father this afternoon. Probably he went to sic her on me.''

She smiled at the exasperation she read in his face, calming now that she

was away from King's disturbing in-
fluence.

She laid a hand on his sleeve.
"She?"

His lips made a thin line. "Mary
Kate Culhane," he said shortly.
"She's two years younger than I am,
and blonde, and she can outrope most
any cowboy. Her father owns the
ranch that adjoins ours. What a great
merging of empires there could be.
And all we have to sacrifice for the
merger is me."

"To Mary Kate Culhane?" she
probed with a grin.

"Exactly." He sighed, glancing at
her sheepishly. "Now you know why
you're here, and why we're engaged."

"Would King really do that?" she
asked solemnly.

"Sure! So would Mom and Dad."

She drew in a quick breath. "I
can't believe it!"

"You don't know what the prospect of mergers and heirs does to normally sane people," he told her, shaking his head. "They know King isn't about to make the supreme sacrifice—not anytime soon, and definitely not with Mary Kate. But I'm the youngest. I'm expendable. I'm the Judas goat."

"Oh, poor boy," she laughed softly.

"You don't know the half of it. But you will tomorrow." He looked down at her, then it suddenly dawned on him that the door to the living room was closed. He glanced toward it, then back at her. "Why are you out here?"

Her slender shoulders lifted and fell helplessly. "Can't you guess?" she asked with wry humor.

"He let you have it, huh?" he asked.

"Both barrels."

"What did he say?"

She stared down at the carpet. "Never mind. It wasn't important," she said softly. Her huge doe eyes went up to Danny's. "He can't help the way he feels, Danny. You don't really have to have reasons for disliking people. And my mother isn't the best character recommendation around."

"You're nothing like your mother," he grumbled.

"King doesn't know that. He doesn't really know me at all, and circumstantial evidence can be damning, as you well know. Anyway, does it matter? He's just upset because I don't belong to your kind of world."

"For God's sake, Shelby, we're not snobs!"

"I know that, Danny, but we move in different circles. My mother's the rich lady, not me, remember? My friends are mostly writers and artists and 'peculiar' people.'' She smiled. ''I like to sit in coffee shops and drink imported coffee at one o'clock in the morning while Edie recites 18th century poetry. Mostly I do that in jeans and a sweatshirt. I wouldn't know what to do at cattle ranching— although I have to admit it fascinates me.''

He smiled. ''We don't have that many parties around here, and I hang out in jeans, myself.''

''The price of one pair of your jeans,'' she teased, ''would buy six pairs of mine.''

He looped his arms around her waist and stared down at her affectionately. ''You,'' he told her, ''are a pain. You've been hanging around Edie for too long.''

''I'm glad we're not really getting married,'' she told him seriously. ''I like you too much.''

He frowned. "You've got some weird ideas about marriage," he said.

"My mother hasn't been too successful at it," she reminded him. "Although it looks like she's going to keep trying until she gets the hang of it," she added with humor that concealed a great hurt. The other children at school had enjoyed teasing her about the number and frequency of her "fathers." It had hurt then, and the years between hadn't lessened the sting. King's cold remark about it tonight had brought it all back, and she felt like the lonely little girl hiding behind chairs at cocktail parties.

"Don't look so sad," Danny said gently. "I won't leave you alone with King again. It'll all be over before you know it, and once I've got Mary Kate out of the picture, I'll tell everybody the truth about us. Fair enough?"

She smiled. "Fair enough."

He bent and kissed her gently on the forehead, just as the sound of a door opening broke into the companionable silence.

"It's one in the morning," King said coolly. "Why don't you two go to bed and do that in private?"

Danny scowled at him. "We don't sleep together," he said gruffly.

One dark eyebrow went up. "No?" he asked with a pointed glance at Shelby. "I'm surprised. I thought models were liberated."

Shelby pulled away from Danny. "I'll see you in the morning," she told him softly, ignoring King with a graceful dignity far beyond her years. "Goodnight."

"Goodnight, honey," Danny said.

She felt King's eyes as she went up the stairs. Angry voices were coming from the hall when she reached the top.

* * *

She slept fitfully, waking long before the housekeeper, Mrs. Denton, came to rouse her for breakfast.

"I'll bet I've seen every movie your mother ever made," the buxom housekeeper said enthusiastically, leading the way downstairs with her heavy, ambling tread. "She's a very good actress."

"Thank you," Shelby murmured, her eyes on the housekeeper's broad back.

"I guess it was fun having a famous actress for a mother," she continued conversationally. She led Shelby into the dining room. "I'll bet you had everything you wanted."

"Everything," Shelby said dully, remembering the lonely vacations at camp, the holidays with only the household staff for company, the birthdays without a cake or a party, childhood illnesses that a nurse got her through because her beautiful mother couldn't stand to be around sick people.

That deep sadness was still in her eyes when she looked up unexpectedly into King's dark, impassive face and felt the ground fall out from under her. Her heart jumped wildly, and sensations ran through her slender body that she'd never felt and couldn't begin to understand.

"Rough night?" he asked pointedly.

She averted her face and took a seat at the table as far away from him as the china table settings would permit.

"I slept very well, thank you," she said softly.

"Damn you, what does it take to get through that steel webbing you wear around your emotions?" he growled, catching her shoulder painfully to jerk her around.

She looked up at him, and her

lower lip trembled, her whole body trembled with the force of the fear he aroused in her. Her eyes misted with tears as they met his, feeling his hand tighten on her soft flesh with a sense of panic.

His touch burned, excited—her eyes were drawn unconsciously to the bronzed glimpse of his broad chest where his blue silk shirt was unbuttoned. A shadowing of dark, curling hair was visible under its thinness, the hard muscles of his arms emphasized by the tight fit as his powerful legs were outlined by the close-fitting blue cord slacks he was wearing. There was something sensuously masculine about him, even though he gave the appearance of a man who was totally devoid of passion. Shelby wondered idly if he was as cold as he seemed to be; if that was the reason he'd lost the woman he cared for.

''You're hurting me, King,'' she

breathed, finally aware of the vice-like grip he had on her thin shoulder.

He loosened his hold, although he didn't move his hand. "I'm not surprised," he said in a goaded tone. "You're like porcelain to touch. A strong wind would blow you all the way back to San Antonio."

"Fat models aren't in vogue this year," she murmured absently.

Surprisingly, his chiseled mouth turned up imperceptibly at the corners. "Aren't they?"

Her eyes searched his, but she couldn't read them. "King...?"

His gaze dropped to her soft mouth, studying it with an intensity that was disturbing. "You aren't wearing makeup," he observed, frowning as if it surprised him.

"I only wear it when I have to," she said quietly. "I...I don't like artificial things."

That seemed to surprise him even

more, but before he could pursue it, footsteps and voices sounded in the hall.

A minute later, Danny came in grinning, followed by Jim and Kate Brannt, to find King and Shelby sitting quietly apart at the table.

When breakfast was over, Danny threw down his napkin. "Well," he said, "I think Shelby and I will head on over to town and get a good seat before the parade gets underway."

"Oh, but hell, no, you won't," King said pleasantly. "We're all going together. And I thought Mary Kate Culhane was expected," he added narrowly.

"Now, look, King..." Danny began hotly.

"Danny, you know Mary Kate always goes to the fiesta with us," Kate Brannt told her son gently. She smiled. "Besides, Mary Kate's been so looking forward to meeting Shelby.''

That, Shelby thought, sounded ominous. She had visions of having to fend off a jealous rival as well as King, and all of a sudden she wanted to develop a migraine and forget the whole thing.

"You'll enjoy the chili cookoff, Shelby," Jim told her over his coffee cup. "Best damned chili in Texas comes out of it, and they even supply the water to put the fire out with!" He laughed.

"Jim's one of the judges," Kate explained. "He doesn't have taste buds any more, they've all been burned off."

"I'm not surprised," Shelby smiled.

"The most fun, though, is the river race," Jim told her. "You've never seen such a conglomeration of floats. Everything from life rafts to surfboards to inner tubes. Good thing the river's down this time of year, before the floods come. There are some rapids on the race stretch, and when the river's up, it can get dangerous.''

''Yes, I know,'' Shelby said demurely. ''I used to live in Georgia with my aunt, and there is always a race of some kind on holidays near the Chattahoochee River. I've been down that in an inner tube. I've even shot the white water on the Chattooga River in north Georgia, where it's the most dangerous. I'm a veteran river rat,'' she added with a glance at King that spoke volumes.

''Well, I'll be damned,'' King murmured, and Shelby felt a tingle of pleasure at the genuine surprise that registered for an instant in his dark face.

''I could say something to that,'' Danny said with pointed reference to King's remark, ''but I won't. Mary

Kate said you were over at their place yesterday.''

"I was. Pretty girl, Mary Kate," King added. "Sexy as hell.''

"I don't like sexy women," Danny said loftily. "They cause gout.''

King's eyes narrowed calculatingly. "You don't think Shelby's sexy?'' he asked.

Danny looked caught out. "Of course I do," he said quickly. "But not like Mary Kate. I mean...damn it, King!''

Kate Brannt's dark green eyes met her youngest son's accusingly. "Please don't use hard language at my breakfast table. It gives me indigestion.''

"King does it all the time," Danny protested.

"Kingston also gives me indigestion," Kate replied. "And he knows it," she added with a speaking glance at King.

King smiled at her. It changed him, made him look less formidable, more human; and dangerously attractive.

"Blame Dad," King told his mother. "He taught me how."

Jim Brannt glowered at his son with blazing dark eyes. "The hell I did!" he burst out, and everyone laughed.

Three

Mary Kate Culhane was as slender as a wand, had green eyes, and the personality of a seasoned game show host. She wasn't pretty, but she was vivacious and as friendly as a puppy—to everyone except Shelby. Her first sight of the younger, darker girl was enough to make her green eyes glow like emeralds. She was polite, but there was ice under the smile she gave Shelby when they were introduced.

"So you're Shelby," Mary Kate said, her eyes nipping at the younger girl, looking for faults and turning darker when she found none. "Danny says you're a model."

"That's right," Shelby said quietly.

"What do you model?" Mary Kate persisted.

"Clothes, mostly," the younger girl said with a calm that seemed to make the other catch fire.

"You don't dress like one," Mary Kate replied with a cattiness that only another woman would catch.

"Thank you," Shelby grinned.

That brought a stunned look to the other girl's face, and an amused smile to Danny's.

"I shouldn't think you'd take to ranch life," Mary Kate renewed her attack. "Being used to San Antonio and night life and all. This must be awfully dull to a city person like you.''

King had moved out into the hall and was leaning against the wall smoking a cigarette while he waited for his parents to catch up. He watched the exchange with unreadable eyes.

''Why would I find it dull?'' Shelby blinked.

''Because there's no night life!''

''I'm not a vampire,'' Shelby said kindly.

Mary Kate's tanned face burned suddenly, and King stepped forward before she could continue.

''I think it's time we got on the road,'' he said, ''or we'll miss the damned thing.''

''Oh, lovely, I'm looking forward to introducing Danny to some of the new set here,'' Mary Kate cooed, and took possession of Danny's arm as if she were conquering a town. "Danny, remember old Coach Garner? Well, he's still coaching the band. Do you remember..." and she led Danny out the door, toward the elder Brannts' new luxury compact car.

As Shelby started toward it, too, King suddenly caught her arm and pulled her toward his sleek black Porsche.

"But, the others...Danny!" she protested, pulling futilely against that steely grip.

"Never mind Danny," he said curtly. He opened the door on the passenger side and put her inside.

"King..." she protested again as he got in beside her and cranked the car.

"Just sit still and hush, Shelby," he said coolly. "No way could Dad cram all five of you into that car, despite what he said. I think we can bear each other's company into town, can't we?''

She folded her hands in her lap and stared at them. "I suppose."

"What do you think of Mary Kate?" he asked as he pulled smoothly out of the driveway, not waiting for his parents to get inside their car and follow.

"She's lovely," she said quietly. "Danny's age, too, isn't she, or just about?"

He frowned. His eyes slid sideways, appraisingly. "How old are you?"

"Twenty-one."

He scowled. "Is that all? My God, I thought you were at least twenty-four!"

"I feel twice that, sometimes," she said in a subdued tone, her eyes going dark and sad with memory.

"You're barely old enough to leave home," he growled.

"I left home when I was fourteen," she recalled, cringing inward at the memory of why she'd had to go.

"Fourteen?!"

"I went to live with my aunt in Georgia," she murmured. "She had a home in the mountains, with a stream out back, and lots of mountain laurel and rhododendron...." She remembered suddenly who she was talking to, and the enthusiasm went out of her voice.

"Don't stop," he said. "And what?"

"And deer," she continued. "We used to sit on the back porch and watch them drink from the stream. One was a nine-point buck, and my cousin shot him one November. I cried because he was such a beautiful animal."

"Your cousin?" he taunted.

"No, the *deer*!" she corrected. Her

eyes touched him suspiciously. He wasn't smiling, but there was a suspicious twinkle in his dark eyes.

"Why did you leave home?"

"I...didn't like Hollywood."

"Oh? Most girls would have loved it. Especially with a movie star mother and plenty of money to buy things with," he prodded.

"I suppose," she said tightly.

"And plenty of stepfathers to spoil you," he added.

She felt a tremor go through her slender body. She wrapped her fingers around her forearms, clasped across her chest, and hoped he wouldn't notice the sudden paleness of her face.

"Yes," she said tightly. "Plenty of stepfathers."

He glanced at her. "But not to spoil you," he guessed quietly. "Were they why you had to leave home, little girl?"

She bit her lower lip. "Please, King, please…!"

"Oh, hell, forget it!" he lashed out. He concentrated on maneuvering the turn onto the main highway, his eyes darting right and left as he pulled out smoothly, not even jerking her as he shifted gears on the powerful sports car and accelerated.

"You worry me to death, the way you bottle things up inside you, Shelby," he said after a long silence. "You'll have ulcers one day."

"It's my life," she said softly.

His jaw tautened. "Doesn't Danny care that you sit and let yourself be whipped to death by the world at large?"

"I don't need protecting," she said with a tiny smile.

"Don't you, honey?" he asked roughly. His dark eyes burned over her for an instant. "You're as vulnerable as a butterfly."

"Not so vulnerable," she murmured, remembering how her life had been all those years ago.

"Then why won't you fight back?"

She smiled. "I'm hardly a match for you, am I?"

Something alien flared in his eyes for an instant. "Not at your age, no."

Both her thin eyebrows went up. "I didn't realize you were so old."

He only smiled, if a slight turning up of his chiseled lips could be called that. "You'd be surprised." He glanced at her. "Have you and Danny set a date?"

"Why bother?" she asked. "You told me you weren't going to let us get married."

"Sarcasm, Shelby?" He did smile then. "That's a change."

"I wasn't being sarcastic." She stared at him openly, her eyes touching every hard line of his face.

"King, why don't you want Danny to marry me? Is it because of my background, or because of me?"

His face hardened. "Remind me to tell you all about it someday when we've got more time."

She wanted to tell him that it was all a farce, that she and Danny would never have that kind of relationship. But she'd promised Danny not to tell.

"I'm not like my mother," she murmured, and didn't even think he'd heard her.

He pulled into town, quickly whipping the sleek, low car into a parking space just off the street. All around, parade members were getting ready. Band players in Mexican dress were practicing on their instruments. Children in colorful Spanish costumes were dancing around the streets where traffic was already moving at a snail pace. It was truly a festival atmosphere.

King cut the engine and turned toward Shelby. His dark eyes met hers levelly and held them for so long that her complexion went dusky.

"You're just like your mother," he corrected gruffly. "You're her image."

"That's the outside," she replied.

"That's all there is," he said matter-of-factly.

"I'm glad you're so sure of that."

He lit a cigarette, glancing out the windshield to where the local high school band in its colorful Mexican uniforms was lining up in formation. Further away, the Brannt's little white compact car was just pulling into a parking space across the street.

"Parades," King growled. "What a hell of a waste of time."

"Don't you like music?" she asked curiously.

"I like a military band or a symphony orchestra. You haven't had to suffer the brass section of this out-fit,'' he grumbled. ''And I'll be damned if I'm going to. There's an air show out at the airport. I'm going there instead.''

''An air show?'' She didn't realize how her face lit up at the mention of it, or how big and bright her dark eyes became. King looked at her as if he'd only just realized that she was beautiful.

''Don't tell me you like airplanes, young Shelby?'' he murmured.

''My father...my real father,'' she corrected, ''was a pilot. He used to take me up when I was only four years old. He could do anything with a plane,'' she laughed, remembering. ''Barrel rolls, spins, dives...and he didn't even have an aerobatic license. If the FAA had ever caught him...''

King frowned. ''What happened to him?''

The laughter left her dark eyes all

of a sudden. She turned them out the window. "He...he found mother with another man. They had an argument, and he drank heavily that night. Early the next morning, the police came to tell us that he'd crashed his plane into a mountain. Apparently he'd taken it up when we thought he was in bed asleep." She sighed and felt a prickling of hurt at the memory. "It was a long time ago."

"How old were you?"

"Ten."

"But you still love planes."

"He loved them." She clasped her hands in her lap. "He was the only person I cared about for a long time. He was larger than life. Every time I go up in a plane now, I remember him. It's almost like being with him again when I fly. I've had my ground training, but somehow I never got time to get in any hours of flight training."

"My God, you're a puzzle," he said heavily.

"Do you fly?" she asked.

"I have to, honey," he replied quietly. "I spend a lot of time traveling on ranch business."

She nodded, idly watching the smoke from his cigarette curl up in thin gray spirals. His brown fingers drew her attention. He had beautiful, masculine hands—tanned and strong and square-tipped, with dark curling hair on the backs of them traveling up into the sleeves of his shirt.

"Do you really want to watch the parade?" he asked her suddenly.

She shook her head, and her heart ran away with her.

"All right, then." He cranked the car and reversed it.

Danny and Mary Kate Culhane were coming across the street as King pulled out into it. He pressed a button on the door and the window powered down. He called to Danny.

"We're going to the air show," he told his brother. "We'll be back in time for lunch."

Danny's eyebrows went up and Shelby could have sworn his eyes were dancing. "Sure," he said. "We'll see you then."

Mary Kate Culhane had a death grip on the younger Brannt's arm. "Have fun!" she called, with a smug, confident look on her peaches and cream complexioned face.

King didn't even answer her. He turned the car and sped down the road toward the airport. "I must be crazy as hell," he muttered.

"If you don't want me along..." she began.

"Shut up, Shelby," he said flatly. He scowled over his cigarette. "Just because I'm taking you to an air show doesn't mean I've changed my mind, so don't get ideas.''

She sighed. ''I didn't expect that you'd change it,'' she agreed. ''But thank you for this.''

He only went faster, his face like a thunderhead.

The air show was everything Shelby expected it to be. She watched the pilots stall out and do rolls and spins until her head ached, and her neck felt as if it was going to break. But it was delicious, every minute of it.

''Oh, I wish I was up there with them!'' she breathed, her eyes bright with challenge and sheer joy.

King looked down at her from his superior height with narrowed eyes. ''You're full of surprises,'' he said absently. ''Not the tame little lamb you appear to be, are you, Shelby? That part of you's an act, and Danny doesn't even realize it.''

"An act?" she echoed blankly, looking up at him.

"You're a passionate woman," he said flatly. "Your eyes are full of it. Your mouth..." His eyes dropped to it, tracing its softness. "You keep the passion well hidden, but it's there, all the same."

She blushed, turning away. She didn't even answer him.

"Embarrassed?" he asked, moving closer to where they stood at the fence around the airport apron. "Why?"

"I...I wish you wouldn't...."

"You run every time I mention intimate relationships," he said quietly. "The last time, you ran away in the middle of the night and had the whole household in an uproar worrying about you."

She blushed even more, and her fingers clenched inward until the knuckles turned white. "What you said about me that night...it wasn't true!'' she whispered.

''I don't remember saying anything about you,'' he replied frankly. ''I invited you into my bed, you said 'no', and I left you standing on the stairs.''

Her eyes closed on the memory. He'd looked at her that night as if she'd been a slave girl on auction, his eyes insolent and calculating. She hadn't dared tell Danny what happened. After all, King was the brother he worshipped. She couldn't tear down that image. But it was what King had said that hurt the most— ''Your mother wouldn't have said no,'' he'd taunted sarcastically. ''You won't fool me with that virginal act, either, Shelby. I'll bet you've given out a dozen times before tonight, so why not me?''

But she'd refused him, and he'd never know how it had cut her, that cold-blooded proposition he'd made without even touching her. She could still almost hate him for it.

There was a long, tight silence between them. "Anything could have happened to you that night, alone on the highway after midnight," he said in a voice she didn't recognize. "My God, how could you have been so stupid, Shelby?"

"I only wanted to get away from you," she said in a low voice. "I'd have walked through hell to get away from you that night."

A shadow passed across his face, but he didn't answer her. He threw his half-smoked cigarette to the ground and crushed it under the heel of his dress boot. "I've had enough. Let's go."

She followed him back to the car and got in beside him. The sense of comradeship that had lasted between them for such a short time was gone again; this time, perhaps for good.

Four

Shelby sat with Danny at lunch, eating barbecue under the Spanish moss beards of the towering live oaks. Across the way, at the table with Jim and Kate Brannt, Mary Kate Culhane was shooting poisonous glances in Shelby's direction.

"You're not enjoying yourself," Danny said gently. "Did King start on you again?"

"Did King ever stop?" she asked with soft laughter. "I don't know what possessed me to go with him to the air show, or why he asked me. We're like soda and vinegar...."

"Or fire and wind," Danny teased. His green eyes probed hers. "Give it a chance, Shelby."

She frowned. "Give what a chance?"

He looked vaguely uncomfortable and quickly changed the subject. "Did you enjoy the air show?"

"Most of it, yes. Danny...?"

"Please look lovingly at me," he pleaded, darting a glance toward the other table. "Mary Kate is really turning on the charm. Don't sacrifice me—!"

"Oh, you crazy man," she laughed. She laid a hand on his forearm. "Danny, I do like you."

He grinned. "I like you, too. Don't

let King upset you. He improves on closer acquaintance.''

''You told me that two years ago, and it hasn't happened yet,'' she reminded him.

''You haven't gotten close enough yet.''

Her eyes darkened. ''I don't want to,'' she said fervently.

''Are you afraid of him, Shelby?''

She looked up. ''Terrified!'' she admitted. ''Danny, don't leave me alone with him again.''

''Honey, I'm trying,'' he laughed. ''It's just that Mary Kate keeps...''

''You're going to miss the river race,'' King said, coming up beside them with a can of beer in one lean hand.

''Can't let that happen, can we?'' Danny chuckled. He picked up their refuse and took it over to a nearby garbage can, leaving her with King.

''What do I do about an inner

tube?'' she asked him conversationally.

"Forget it," he bit off. His jaw tautened. "You're not going to kill yourself in the river to prove anything."

"But, King…!"

"Scratches on that perfect skin would put you out of work, wouldn't they?" he asked with an uncanny insight.

She glared down at her sandaled feet. "That seems to bother everybody more than it bothers me," she said tightly. "I'm not made of glass. I don't care if I get scratched."

"Nice try, honey," he said with a cold smile. "But I'm not that dense. Save the act for Danny. He's young enough to be taken in by it."

She started to argue, but what was the use? He'd never change his mind about her. She turned to Danny and slid her arm through his as he came back from emptying the trash. He smiled down at her.

"Still want to get in the river?" he teased.

"She's not racing," King said firmly, his dark eyes meeting his brother's doggedly. "It's too risky."

"Tell her, not me," Danny laughed. "I'm not that much of a daredevil. Now, he is," Danny told Shelby, jerking a thumb toward his elder brother. "He'd scare you to death in a canoe."

"I wonder," King said narrowly, studying Shelby in earnest.

"Oh, Danny!" Mary Kate called, moving forward to capture the arm Shelby didn't have a claim on. "Would you get into the three-legged race with me? I don't have a partner." She made it sound like a federal offense.

Danny looked at Shelby apologetically. "Do you mind?" he asked, but Mary Kate was already dragging him away.

"I thought you were engaged to him?" King murmured, and there was a glimmer of amusement in his eyes. He drained the can of beer and tossed it into a nearby trash can.

Shelby clasped her hands behind her, staring at the retreating couple and smiled wistfully at her only source of protection as it was shanghaied away. "A willful girl is Mary Kate Culhane," she murmured. "You planned this, didn't you, King?"

"Hell, yes," he admitted shamelessly. "Mary Kate has something to offer."

"Indeed she does," Shelby agreed quietly. "A sixteen thousand acre ranch with a herd of purebred Santa Gertrudis cattle, oil rights, and three real estate companies. And all I have to offer," she added in a subdued tone, "is a common background, a career that ends when I reach thirty or thereabout, and an infamous mother." She turned away, feeling the hurt all the way to the bone, as if she'd really been promised in marriage to Danny, as if it were real.

"Shelby," he said quietly.

She stopped, but she didn't turn.

"She loves him," King said quietly. "You don't. Not in a way you should to be considering marriage."

Did he really see that deep, she wondered incredulously. She swallowed. "How do you know what I feel?"

"Last night when I came out of the living room, he was kissing you on the forehead," he replied. "That told me all I needed to know."

She turned, meeting his solemn gaze. "I don't understand."

"If you were engaged to me, there wouldn't be any chaste little kisses on the forehead, Shelby," he said tautly. "I'd take your mouth and have you begging me for more. And we wouldn't be sleeping in separate bedrooms."

Her face flamed, but she didn't take her eyes away. "You flatter yourself," she said shakily.

"I said 'if,' honey," he reminded her coolly. "I wouldn't take you with an oil well thrown in."

She turned away from him.

"Running away?" he taunted. "Where to now?"

"To get an inner tube," she said through her teeth.

"Oh, hell, no, you don't!" he bit off. He moved forward, catching her arm in a steely, painful grasp and whirled her around so that he could see her mutinous young face.

"Let go of me," she said tightly. "You aren't my keeper!"

His eyes narrowed and became

searching. "Did I hit a nerve, honey?"

"Please don't call me that," she said, averting her eyes as she stiffened in his grasp. "You make it sound cheap."

His fingers tightened. "Aren't you?"

"Leave me alone," she pleaded in a broken whisper, closing her eyes on the sight of that darkly tanned hand wrapped around her small wrist. "Please, King, can't you just leave me alone!"

"I wish to God I could," he growled enigmatically. He let go of her wrist. "You'll stay with me, young Shelby. I'll be damned if I'm letting you near the water."

"Afraid I might win?" she taunted, darting a tremulous glance in his direction as he fell into step beside her.

He glanced down at her with an

unreadable expression in his dark eyes. "I just might be," he said quietly.

Danny hadn't come downstairs when Shelby got to the breakfast table the next morning, earlier than the rest of the family. King was still there, just folding his morning paper as he finished the last of his coffee and reached for the pot to refill it.

He looked up as she froze in the doorway.

"Don't start backing up, baby," he remarked softly. "It's too late now."

She moved to the table and sat down gingerly, feeling every muscle in her body tense as he stared at her, at the picture she made in her white blouse and slacks, complementing her darkness. He was wearing work clothes this morning; blue denim that was expensively cut, but still had the look of utility. His shirt was open halfway down the front and his bronzed chest was damp, as if he'd already been outside in the heat.

"Danny's not up yet?" he asked casually.

"I don't know," she murmured, reaching for the cup of coffee he poured and handed to her. An impish smile touched her mouth as she took the china cup and saucer in hand. "I think he's recuperating from Mary Kate Culhane."

He actually laughed, a sound so rare it brought her curious eyes up to meet his.

"Maybe he is." He tossed down the rest of his coffee. "Want to come watch us brand cattle, city lady?"

She gaped at him. "Could I?" she asked incredulously.

"Not in that gear," he replied, frowning at her white clothes. "You'll need jeans and thick socks, boots, and a blouse that won't show dirt. And," he added darkly, "Danny's permission, if you can get it."

"Danny won't mind," she said without thinking.

"I'd mind if you belonged to me," he said flatly. "I'd mind like hell."

"You aren't Danny," she reminded him softly. "If you mean it, I'll go and change."

He glanced at the wide leather band that held his watch in place. "I mean it for the next twenty minutes. After that, I'm gone."

"I'll be ready," she promised. She dug into her breakfast with an appetite that would have done credit to an athlete after a 20 mile hike.

She met him at the corral, neatly dressed in a pair of faded jeans and a yellow tank top, without makeup, her eyes sparkling.

He frowned down at her. "Just like

a cowgirl," he murmured. "And still no makeup. Don't I rate it, or do you really prefer to go without it?"

She dropped her eyes. "I don't have any reason to try and attract your attention, King," she reminded him. "And even if I did, I don't like pretentiousness."

"God, what a word!" he chuckled.

"I told you before I didn't like artificial things," she replied as she followed him to the horse he'd saddled for her—a young Appaloosa filly.

"Neither do I, honey, but you'll have to do more than go without makeup to convince me."

"Why bother?" she asked quietly. "You enjoy believing the worst."

He raised an eyebrow and stood looking down at her as he lifted the filly's reins to the pommel of the saddle. "You might change my mind if you worked at it," he said in a low, deep voice that sent shivers down her spine.

She stared at him, her heart almost shaking her with its pounding as she met the look in those dark, deep-set eyes.

"Don't panic," he said softly, and a thin smile touched his hard mouth. "You're safe enough—for the moment."

He put her up on the filly and mounted his own black stallion gracefully, reining in alongside her as they rode out. She couldn't manage to look at him just yet. That curious look in his eyes had drained her of courage.

"Where did you get the hat?" he asked after a minute, his eyes flicking to the brown suede hat sitting jauntily atop her ebony hair.

"Your mother loaned it to me," she murmured. She glanced at him. "I thought roundup and all was left to the ranch manager," she murmured, desperate to find a safe topic of conversation.

"Jim Deyton runs things when Dad and I are away," he agreed, narrowing his eyes as he watched cattle grazing in the distance. "And I've got a man who takes care of the purebred stock full time."

"One man to do nothing but that?" she exclaimed.

He glanced at her and a pale smile touched his hard mouth. "You don't know much about cattle, do you, honey? How much do you think that seed bull of mine is worth—the Santa Gertrudis?"

She blinked, "Oh, probably at least a thousand dollars," she said.

"Try a quarter of a million."

"*Dollars?!*" she choked.

"Dollars. We own sixty-two percent of him. Brownland Farms owns the other thirty-eight percent."

She sighed heavily. "My gosh, I didn't realize one bull was worth all that much money."

"That particular bull damned well is. He's sired six champions, and he came from a foundation herd sale on the ranch a few counties over." He glanced at her. "I imagine you know the one?"

"Anybody who knows Texas knows that one," she admitted. "Even if they don't know cattle."

"You could learn. You already like the ranch, don't you, city lady?"

She nodded, casting her eyes around at the gently rolling countryside, the shadows of trees on the long horizon. "It's so peaceful here."

"It's that, all right. And there's plenty of elbow room. I like walking around without running into things," he said.

"But you do occasionally spend time in the city," she reminded him.

"I have to. This ranch is a corporation, not an empire. And we have other holdings as well—oil, real estate...I'm a business executive more than a cattleman."

"You just prefer cattle."

"That's a fact, honey. I like them better than people most of the time," he added with a taunting smile.

"You don't have to rub it in," she said quietly, nudging her mount into a canter.

He grabbed the bridle and brought her up short, his eyes boring into hers. "I didn't mean you. Stop bristling at me, Shelby, I wasn't making fun of you."

She flushed. "You do most of the time."

He scowled. "Do I?" he asked, and there was genuine curiosity in his tone.

"I know you don't like me," she replied, clutching the leather-covered pommel for dear life, "and you don't think I'm good enough for Danny, but couldn't you just..."

"Hold it right there," he said grimly. "Who the hell said I don't think you're good enough for my brother?"

"It's the way you treat me, as if..."

"I don't want you to marry him, that's so," he admitted. "But your background doesn't have a damned thing to do with it. You're a world away from Danny. You don't even like the same things. My God, he wouldn't go near a river, and you like to shoot the white water. He only looks reckless, but you are. You like bucking the odds. I can see it now. Danny would be home watching television while you were out hang-gliding down some mountain. You've got nothing in common except that you like each other. Hell, Shelby,

Danny doesn't even like children, had you thought about that?''

''No,'' she said honestly, not bothering to tell him she hadn't because it didn't matter since she wasn't really marrying Danny.

''Do you want children?'' he asked.

She stared at him, and the words came out without volition. ''Oh, yes,'' she said softly. There was an intensity in King's eyes that she couldn't understand. ''Do you?'' she asked without knowing why.

He nodded, his face somber. His eyes swept over her slowly, appraisingly. ''You're not built for babies.''

''That doesn't mean I couldn't have them.''

''No,'' he agreed. ''A woman who isn't afraid of white water wouldn't be afraid of childbirth. But would you take to life on a cattle ranch? It's damned lonely here. There aren't any nightclubs or boutiques.''

''Do I need them?'' she asked wistfully.

''You tell me. You're a model.''

''Yes, I am,'' she agreed dully. ''A walking, talking eight by ten glossy.''

He scowled at her, but he didn't pursue it. ''Let's get moving, honey, I've got a long day ahead.''

He hurried her around the corrals where the branding and vetting of cattle was being done, as if he was suddenly anxious to get rid of her. It all became a maze of dust and heat and bawling cattle and burning hide. He took her back to the ranch house after a whirlwind tour of the cattle operation and left her with barely a word.

She spent the rest of the afternoon with the elder Brannts, trying her best not to appear concerned that Danny had gone off with Mary Kate Culhane for the day. Strange, she thought, how Danny was pointedly calling attention to his attraction for Mary Kate and his lack of real interest in Shelby. Especially since the fake engagement had been his idea. Shelby couldn't begin to fathom his reasoning. Neither could King, apparently. When he was told at the supper table that Danny was having supper with the Culhanes, he speared a glance at Shelby, threw down his napkin and left the room.

She couldn't sleep that night. Her nerves were all on edge, raw. It was because of King, because of the way he affected her. She'd always been aware of his physical attractions, but she'd managed to keep her feelings carefully camouflaged before. Now it was getting harder by the day not to let them show. She caved in when she was around him. The air show yesterday, the unexpected bonus of spending a morning with him today, had left her with a glow she never expected. He made her pulses run wild just by looking at her. But she felt, ironically, incredibly safe with him. Secure. Protected. She rolled over with a sigh. Why did she have to feel like this about King, anyway? Why couldn't she have felt that way about Danny instead?

King didn't want any part of her, that was for sure. All he wanted was for Shelby to get out of his brother's life so that there'd be room for Mary Kate in it. Mary Kate with her cattle and oil that would give King and his father an even bigger empire and the hope of an heir to leave it to.

She pounded the pillow in its cool, crisp pillowcase and tossed restlessly onto her side. Why hadn't she been born a country girl? Maybe then King would at least tolerate her. But she was a "city lady" and he wasn't going to forget that.

With a moan of frustration, she swung her feet to the floor and pulled on her burgundy dressing gown. She flicked on the small light by her bed and yawned. She just wasn't sleepy, and there was no forcing it. Maybe if she had a book to read...

She went downstairs carefully, only able to see by the muted light of the wall lamps along the staircase, and into the den. Her bare feet didn't make any noise at all on the thick pile of the carpet. She was careful to leave the door slightly ajar, too, so there wouldn't be any unnecessary noise.

Her slender hands touched the covers of the fiction books in the soft light that came from the desk lamp, but none of the titles interested her. She moved along to the nonfiction portion of the shelf and discovered a volume on Western history. She tugged it out carefully and leafed through it, her eyes fascinated by actual photographs of such infamous Westerners as John Henry "Doc" Holliday and Cole Younger. She was lost in the book when she felt a sudden prickling sensation at the back of her neck. She turned around and gasped when she saw King standing just inside the door, scowling at her.

His shirt was unbuttoned, hanging loose from his trousers, baring his bronzed, muscular chest with its heavy wedge of curling dark hair. His hair was mussed, as if he'd been running his fingers through it. He looked alarmingly masculine and vibrant, and more than just a little dangerous.

"I...I'm not stealing the family silver, if that's what you're worried about," she said, hating the breathless note in her voice.

"Couldn't you sleep, honey?" he asked quietly.

She moistened her dry lips. "No," she admitted. "I thought I might read for a while."

He shouldered away from the door and came toward her, his face dark and unsmiling. He stopped just in front of her, his eyes taking in the quick rise and fall of her breasts under the satin robe, the runaway pulse at the base of her throat.

"I...I'd better get back to bed," she whispered.

His eyes traveled down the length of her slender body lingering where the lapels parted over her thin gown.

"Did you plan on reading yourself to sleep?" he asked.

Not trusting her voice with him this close, she only nodded.

He reached out and took the book from her nerveless hands, idly checking the title with a faint smile before he tossed it onto the desk and caught her by the waist.

"I can think of something that'll put you to sleep a lot faster than reading a book," he murmured sensuously. He pulled her against him slowly, gently, watching the staggering effect it had on her when her slender body touched his.

She caught her breath at the newness of the action, at the feel of his possessive hands on her waist, burning even through the layers of fabric.

"Please don't..." she pleaded in a whisper.

His own breath was coming as quick as hers now. He brushed his open mouth against her forehead. "Run your hands over my chest, Shelby," he whispered gruffly.

She flushed like a schoolgirl. Her fingers clenched where they rested against his cool shirt. "No!"

"You sound like an outraged virgin," he murmured, "and that's

something we both know you're
not.''

"You don't know anything about
me,'' she choked, pushing helplessly
against the rock-hard muscles of his
chest.

"I know what I do to you.'' His
hands moved caressingly against her
waist and back through the robe. "I
can feel it, just as I felt it yesterday
afternoon; this morning. I make you
uneasy as hell, don't I, honey?''

Her head bowed and her heart
raced. "Don't,'' she breathed.

He laughed softly. "What are you
afraid of—betraying Danny? He
wasn't concerned about betraying
you when he went off with Mary
Kate two days in a row, was he?''

"It's just friendship...'' she protested weakly.

"The hell it is.'' He tipped her
chin up and brushed his hard mouth
across her closed eyes. "But if you

don't want Danny to know, we won't tell him.'' His hands came up to cup her flushed young face. He bent and she felt, helplessly, the warm, to-bacco-scented breath on her lips. ''I'll make it good for you, Shelby,'' he whispered sensuously.

His mouth broke against hers, tak-ing it softly, slowly, so that she could feel each slow, deliberate movement of his hard, warm lips, his tongue as it traced the inner line of her mouth. She trembled, and he felt that, too; the soft movement of his lips told her so.

He was no boy. He knew exactly the moves to make that would check her tentative struggles. He was slow and tender and expertly demanding, and Shelby thought that there had never been such a kiss as this, that drained her of will, that made her weak and yielding, that brought her heart trembling into her throat. Her slender hands moved softly across his hard chest and she moaned unconsciously.

King's cool, rough hands left her face and slid down her back to her hips to hold her even closer and, instinctively, she stiffened and tried to pull away from the intimate contact.

He drew back, the question in his dark, scowling expression. He looked down at her as if he'd been stung. He bent again, forcing her mouth open this time, penetrating it roughly, and, again, she flinched away from him, frightened. His lean hand came up to hover over the soft singing line of her breast and she strained away from it, with her heart trying to jump out of her body at the new intimacy of a relationship she'd tried desperately not to let happen between them.

Her apprehensive eyes met his and he blinked, moving his hands into her thick, short hair to hold her face up to his. His eyes were dark and strange, his face like stone, giving nothing away as he studied her.

"Shelby," he whispered breathlessly. His eyes dropped to her soft, tremulous mouth. His thumbs edged out toward her flushed cheeks caressingly. "There's nothing to be afraid of, little girl," he said finally, gently. "I won't force you."

Her stunned eyes asked the question for her.

"Oh, yes, I know," he answered, and he searched her face with a shattering intensity. "I've had too many women not to know. You're very innocent, little one. As lovely as you are, I'm surprised there hasn't been a string of men behind you. But you've never even been held intimately until now, with me."

Her eyes dropped to his bronzed, hair-covered chest between the open edges of the shirt. And never wanted to be held intimately, until now, she could have told him. She wanted to run her fingers over that broad chest and taste his mouth the way he'd been tasting hers. She wanted things of him and with him that she'd never wanted with anyone else, and she was just beginning to realize it.

"I tried to tell you…" she faltered.

"Actions speak louder than words," he reminded her. He reached down and brought her cool, nervous hands against the blazing warmth of his bare skin, moving them into the nest of thick hair. "This is how I like to be touched by a woman," he said against her forehead.

Her hands trembled under his insistent fingers and she was afraid of what he might ask of her in this lonely, dimly lit room; afraid of what she might say or do.

"King," she pleaded breathless,

with one last rush of sanity, "I'm engaged...."

"If he cares so damned much, why did he spend the day with Mary Kate?" he asked roughly. "Why did you spend the morning with me? Stop talking, Shelby. I want to make love to you."

She raised her face to protest and his mouth went down against her parted lips, easing them even farther apart under the coaxing, deepening pressure, drawing gently back when she stiffened, increasing the intensity again when she relaxed. Her hands spread out on his chest, loving the masculine feel of him against her, loving the sensations he was causing in the warm, pulsating silence. She should stop him, she should go back to bed, she told herself. But she was with King, and she wanted the taste and touch of him to last forever.

"You're soft," he whispered

against her trembling mouth, "and warm, and I love the feel of you under my hands, the silky taste of your lips under my mouth. I love the touch of you against my skin. Oh, God, I want you, Shelby!"

Her forehead dropped against the dampness of his chest while she tried to catch her breath, feeling the swollen throb of her mouth with a sense of awe. "I...I can't," she whispered shakily.

"Why not?" he murmured. "It has to start somewhere. Why not with me? You're too passionate to remain so innocent for long. Just like your mother, no man's ever going to satisfy you completely, but I might come close...."

She tore out of his arms and backed away, her eyes full of the sudden mockery in his level gaze, the faint lines of contempt deepening around the mouth she'd kissed so hungrily.

"You needn't look so shocked," he said in a strange tone. "It isn't the first time I've invited you into my bed."

"No," she agreed, hurting, "but it's going to be the last. I'm going home, and this time I won't come back!"

"And what's Danny going to say about that?" he asked contemptuously. He threw a faint smile at her while he lit a cigarette, and she watched him silently, noticing the mussed hair her fingers had tousled, the swell of his lower lip where hers had clung. It embarrassed her a little to remember how completely she'd responded to his rough ardor.

"I don't care what he says," she managed.

"I do." His eyes darkened menacingly. "You walk out that door again like you did the last time, and I'll make your life hell, Shelby. You're not running out on Danny. You're going to tell him the truth. Or I will.''

''And what is the truth?''

''That you want me,'' he said bluntly. ''That I could have you any time I wanted you.''

''That isn't true!'' she cried, horrified.

''The hell it isn't.'' His gaze dropped to her mouth and an unreadable expression flickered for an instant in his eyes. ''If it wasn't for the respect I have for my brother, you'd be in my bed right now, and you damned well know it!''

Her eyes closed under a wave of anguish, because she did know it. Her small hands clenched at her sides and she felt a wave of shame washing over her in the silence that throbbed between them. She could feel King's eyes on her downcast face.

"You think of some way out of this farce of an engagement, Shelby," he told her, "and you do it before you and Danny leave the ranch. You know by now that I don't make threats. If you don't break the engagement, I'll tell him the truth. And you won't like what comes next."

Mutinously, her big dark eyes met his with a rare flash of spirit. "And what's that?" she asked bravely.

"I'll finish what we started here tonight," he replied with deadly confidence. "And I promise you he won't want what I leave of you."

Her face went beet red. "You brute!" she whispered brokenly.

"Even when you fight back, you're lukewarm," he scoffed. "Is that the most insulting thing you can think of to call me?"

"No!" she replied.

He smiled unpleasantly. He crushed out his cigarette in the ashtray on his desk. "I may make a woman out of you yet," he laughed softly. "Come on, Shelby, bed. I'm tired even if you aren't, and I've got a hard day ahead of me."

She flushed. "I won't!"

"Why, Miss Kane," he said with mock surprise, "what did you think I was suggesting?"

Flushing, she whirled and ran out of the room and back up the stairs, hating him as she'd never hated anyone before.

Five

Shelby didn't see King all the next morning. Danny remarked casually that his big brother had flown to Austin on business and wouldn't be back for at least a couple of days.

Shelby breathed a sigh of relief. After last night, it was going to take some time for her to even be able to look King in the face again. How could she have yielded to him so eagerly? Surely she could have held out against his charm if she'd tried...

Who was she kidding? She fell into step beside Danny as they walked through the rose garden behind the house, heading toward the river. She wanted King in a way she'd never be able to want another man, and he knew it. Even now she could feel the hard, warm crush of his mouth, the strength of his arms, and she felt as if she'd been torn in half, missing him already. Was it going to be like this from now on when he was out of her sight? Why did she feel this way? It was almost as if she was in love...

In love. A torrent of emotion raged through her as she savored the words. In love. With King? With a man who'd been nothing but an enemy from the day they'd met, who'd hurt her at every turn, who'd admitted that he'd do anything to keep her from marrying his brother. Last night had just been part of his overall plan to tear her away from Danny. He'd admitted as much. So why did she feel this aching hunger to be in his arms again?

"Oh, King," she whispered breathlessly as the pain surged up in her.

"What?" Danny asked absently.

"Nothing," she replied. "Tell me about the flood they had here last year."

But before Danny could open his mouth, a familiar honeyed voice called out, "Oh, there you are, Danny! Do you think your fiancee would let me borrow you for a few hours?" Mary Kate Culhane asked with a cold glance in Shelby's direction. "I need some legal advice."

"I really shouldn't leave the ranch, Mary Kate," Danny said with a smile. "King's flying back just for a few hours before he heads back out to that sale in North Georgia, and I need to discuss a few things with him.''

Shelby felt her heart bounce against her ribs. So King's few days away weren't quite started yet. Her pulse ran away and she couldn't keep up with what Danny and Mary Kate were discussing for worrying about how she was going to face King. It wouldn't be the same between them ever again. Not after what she'd felt in his arms. And she wasn't any good at hiding her emotions, she never had been.

''Danny, I'm going home,'' she said suddenly, without preamble, and turned to go back to the house.

He caught her arm. ''Now? But you can't!''

''Danny, don't be that way,'' Mary Kate exclaimed with barely contained glee. ''Shelby knows what's she's doing.''

"Shut up, Mary Kate," Danny shot at her, and for an instant he looked just like King in a bad mood. He turned back to Shelby. "You can't go yet. I...uh, I can't leave to take you!" he finished smugly.

"I'll get a cab. A bus. I'll walk."

"All the way to San Antonio?" he burst out. "Shelby, what's the matter? Afraid to wait until King gets here?"

"What makes you say that?" she choked, paling.

"Brilliant deduction," he said proudly. "And I'm not going to let you mess up my carefully thought out plans. Plans, Shelby, remember?" he asked with a hasty glance toward Mary Kate. "Hmmmm?" he persisted.

"What we thought would work, isn't," she said stubbornly, with a glance of her own toward the puzzled blonde.

"You don't know how well it's working," Danny corrected with a grin. "Be a sport. Two more days, then we'll both go, okay? Deal?"

"Now I know what they mean by plea bargaining," Shelby said wearily, but with a smile. "It's a synonym for blackmail."

"That's libelous," he warned.

"Oh, what are you two talking about?" Mary Kate grumbled.

"Nothing at all," Danny lied. "Want to go for a ride, Mary Kate?" he asked with a grin.

Her small face lit up. "Oh, could we?" Her face fell. "What about your fiancee?" she asked in a subdued tone, and for the first time Shelby saw through those cold green eyes, all the way to a very warm little heart that was hurting terribly. It was staggering. Shelby even understood how she felt, because she was beginning to experience similar feelings every time King came to mind.

"I...I have some phone calls to make," Shelby said quickly. "Do go ahead."

Mary Kate gaped at her. "You—don't mind? Really?"

Shelby smiled. "I don't mind, really. Have fun."

Danny tugged a short lock of straight, silky dark hair. "I hope I can tell you that before long."

She turned away. "I wouldn't bet on it. Why don't you tell Mary Kate the truth?" she asked over her shoulder. "You aren't very convincing, anyway."

Danny chuckled. "Maybe you're right."

Shelby walked the rest of the way back deep in thought. What was Danny up to? Surely not protection from Mary Kate, from the look of it. But...what?

Instead of going straight back to the house, she went down by the river and sat down under one of the huge oaks at the water's edge, leaning back on the grassy bank to listen to the hushed roar of the river.

She crossed her legs in their well-fitting jeans, pushed at the sleeves of her blue print cotton blouse. She loosened a button to let the breeze get to her heated skin and stretched back out on the grass, with her hands under her head. Her eyes closed with a sigh. It was so peaceful here. So quiet and green and cool. In seconds, she was asleep.

She heard her name called a first time, and then a second and third. She thought she was dreaming until she felt the hand on her arm.

She opened her eyes quickly and found Kate Brannt standing over her with relief in every line of her aging face. Around her, the sky was a dusky orange.

"Thank goodness you're all right," Kate sighed. "Danny said you'd started back toward the house when he and Mary Kate went riding, and then when you still hadn't come home after King got here, we sent out the search parties."

Shelby scrambled to her feet, brushing off bits of grass from her slacks and the back of her blouse, her heart tumbling as she picked up on what Kate had said.

"King's home?" she asked apprehensively.

"Oh, my dear," Kate said compassionately, "King's very much home, and turning the air blue, and he's already jumped all over Danny. He's cancelled his Georgia trip."

"Jumped…on Danny? What about?"

"You, Shelby," Kate smiled. "He

was furious because my youngest went off with Mary Kate and left you behind to get lost. Not that he isn't mad because you're lost. He and his ranch hands have been combing the ranch," she added with a grimace, "and when I decided to play a hunch and look down here, he was fixing to change horses. I think we'd better get home fast before the fireworks get any worse."

"Oh, I'm so sorry!" Shelby said genuinely, her face ashen as she dreaded seeing that temper of King's unleashed at her. She was really going to catch hell now. "I'm sorry, I didn't sleep last night and I just meant to close my eyes for a minute...I never meant to fall asleep and cause so much trouble."

"Not so much," Kate said with a secretive smile. "I had a feeling you'd be here. I saw your light on early this morning. Early last morning, too. You don't sleep at all lately, do you, my dear?''

"It really isn't Danny's fault..." she began.

"I know."

"You do?" she blinked.

"Never mind, Shelby, you'll understand it all one of these days," Kate told her. "But right now, we've simply got to get King calmed down."

"Do you think it would help if I wore sack cloth and ashes down to the barn?" Shelby asked tremulously.

"I think it would help more if you didn't go near the barn until my son has a chance to cool down," Kate laughed. "King in a temper is a force to behold."

"I know," she said miserably.

"Yes, I suppose you do." Kate glanced at her. "He does get upset over you, doesn't he?"

"Only for Danny's sake," she

murmured. Her eyes happened to catch a glimpse of movement out of one corner and she felt her knees going weak. King was walking toward them with that slow dangerous stride she remembered so well from her last visit here. His hat was pulled low over his eyes, and even at the distance, she could see the set of his jaw, the anger that lined his dark face.

She stopped at the entrance to the garden, her fingers nervously clutching at a big white rose on its thorny stem.

"Now, King," Kate began as he came up to them.

"Goodbye, Mother," he said curtly.

Kate looked at Shelby apologetically, but she was too wary of King's temper not to do as he asked. She went into the house and closed the door gently behind her.

"You scare everybody, don't

you?'' Shelby asked nervously. She spoke to the front of his half-open tan shirt, not his face. She couldn't bear to meet his eyes.

She swallowed nervously when he didn't answer. She studied the soft, cool petals of the rose, tracing them with her fingers.

''Well?'' she whispered unsteadily. ''Aren't you going to yell at me?''

He still didn't say anything, and she licked her lips nervously as she finally mustered enough courage to lift her eyes up to his. She winced at the expression in those furious dark eyes.

''You might as well let it out before you explode, King,'' she said softly.

''Damn you, Shelby!'' he growled, and his lean hands shot out to grasp her upper arms painfully as he shook her once, hard. ''Do you know how big this ranch is? Do you realize how long we could search until we found you if you got yourself lost for real? Where in hell were you?''

''I...I fell asleep by the river,'' she said unsteadily. ''Oh, please, you're hurting me!''

His jaw clenched, but he loosened his tight hold and took a harsh breath. ''You little fool, I could beat you!''

''Yes, I know. I'm sorry.''

''Sorry,'' he scoffed. ''I had half my men on the range hunting you, after they'd put in a twelve-hour day already, and you're sorry!''

Tears rolled down her cheeks as she lowered her eyes to his chest, the brown print shirt blurring in front of her.

''Don't do that!'' he growled.

But his harsh voice made the tears run all the harder. A sob broke from her lips.

"Shelby," he bit off, "oh, God, honey, don't cry!"

He brought her up close to his arms and held her, rocked her against his hard body, soothing her with words she didn't hear, his hand gentle in her hair. The action surprised her so much that suddenly all the frustrated longing poured out. With a sense of wonder she felt the crush of his arms and pressed even closer.

"You little fool," he murmured at her ear. "We didn't even know where to look, Shelby!"

"I'm sorry, King," she whispered like a disobedient child.

He buried his face in her silky neck, his lips hard and warm against it. "It's one hell of a big ranch, Shelby," he said in a strange, deep voice. "We lost a hand once, during the floods. It was three days before we found his body."

Chills swept over her. "I didn't realize... Oh, King, I didn't mean to upset everybody. I was just so sleepy..."

"Don't you sleep at night, little girl?"

"No. Yes," she corrected quickly. But not quickly enough.

He drew back and looked searchingly into her eyes. His own were bloodshot, and there were weary, worn lines in his hard face, as if he hadn't had much sleep himself.

His gaze dropped to her mouth and his hands, where they rested on her back, became subtly caressing. "I didn't sleep last night, either, Shelby," he said quietly.

She flushed at the memory and pressed her cold hands against him.

"What is it?" he asked deeply.

"Danny..."

"Let Danny look out for himself," he said gruffly. "He's so damned wrapped up in Mary Kate, he can't see you for dust, and you know it. Why the hell don't you give him back the ring, Shelby?''

With a thrill of pleasure she felt his arms contract around her, and she lifted her head to look into his deep-set dark eyes.

His glance flickered over her face and then down to her mouth again. ''You burned for me,'' he whispered sensuously. ''Like a candle flame touched by wind.''

Her face reddened, but she didn't lower her face. ''You... Danny said you were going to Austin.''

''I turned around and came back,'' he said. He glanced over her shoulder and back down at her again. ''I couldn't stay away from you.''

Her eyes widened. ''From...me?'' she whispered.

''From you,'' he murmured. ''You missed me, didn't you, honey?''

She met his level gaze shyly.

"Yes," she admitted breathlessly. "King..."

He drew her body relentlessly against his. "Don't tell me," he said softly, "show me."

He teased her lips apart with slow mastery, building the pressure until she moaned with hunger, until she went up on tiptoe to tempt him into increasing it even more, her body arching, aching, as it sought his, her mouth hungry and trembling, her voice breaking on a sobbing moan as it echoed the deep pleasure he was giving her.

King tore away abruptly and lifted an eyebrow as he looked over her head. His face was as hard as ever, completely unmoved by the hunger in the kiss they'd shared. That registered somewhere in the back of Shelby's whirling mind even as she heard his voice as if through a great distance.

"Did you want something?" he asked conversationally.

Danny's smooth voice replied, "Only my fiancee."

Shelby felt her heart stop. She pulled shakily out of King's embrace and turned, darting a shy glance at Danny, who looked for all the world as if he was trying to keep from laughing. But he composed himself quickly and moved closer.

"Are you sure she wants to go with you?" King asked arrogantly.

Everything began to make terrifying sense as she saw the glitter of triumph in King's dark eyes. All of this was for Danny's benefit. It was hitting below the belt, but it seemed he'd go to any lengths to keep her from marrying his brother, even if it meant making her fall headlong in love with him. And she'd done exactly that, she realized with a cold chill. She'd fallen into a carefully baited trap before she ever realized it.

Gathering the shreds of her pride, she lifted her head proudly. "Tell him, Danny," she said gently. "If you don't, I will," she threatened when he hesitated.

Danny sighed heavily, as if the timing didn't suit him. "All right." He met his brother's puzzled eyes. "Shelby and I aren't engaged, King."

King's hard face grew even harder. His eyes narrowed. "You're what?"

"Not engaged." Danny stuck his hands in his pockets, looking faintly sheepish. "I engineered it to keep you people from flinging Mary Kate at my head. I thought that if you thought I was already engaged, you'd get off my back. Mary Kate's okay, but I'm not ready to get married yet."

King looked as if he wanted to hit something. His eyes flashed fire.

"Why the hell didn't you say so, then?" he demanded fiercely.

"What's wrong, brother mine?" Danny taunted. "Frustrated because I didn't throw a punch at you for kissing my girl?"

"From where I was standing," King said tightly, "It looked as if she was doing the kissing."

A muffled sob broke from Shelby's lips. "Oh, you beast," she whispered achingly, her eyes accusing and hurt as they met King's.

"What's the matter, honey, does the truth hurt?" he asked mockingly, his smile more an insult than the words.

"King!" Danny growled.

"Stay out of it," the older man said curtly. His eyes pinned Shelby. "Why don't you go the hell back to the city where you belong? The joke's over, and it's on you, honey. I'm just grateful I don't have to waste any more time on you to make Danny come to his senses!''

With a gasp of shame, she turned and ran into the house. Danny glared at his brother.

''Was that really necessary?'' he asked gruffly.

''What the hell were you trying to do, Danny?'' King demanded, ignoring the question. ''You've been halfway in love with Mary Kate for years. What was this charade in aid of, to draw my attention to Shelby? I don't want her! I never did! So why the hell don't you mind your own damned business, and keep your nose out of mine!''

''King, let me explain...'' Danny began.

''Go to hell,'' was the cold reply. King turned on his heel and stalked off.

Six

It was Saturday afternoon when Shelby walked into the apartment, tired and haggard, her eyes red-rimmed from crying. Edie was in the kitchen and came out smiling into the living room, but one look at Shelby's worn face wiped the smile clean.

"Oh, Shelby, not again," her friend wailed sympathetically, and threw her arms around Shelby. "I'm sorry!"

"So am I," Shelby wept. "I wish I'd listened to you."

"What happened?"

"It's a long story."

"I've got nothing but time," Edie said. "Come have some coffee and tell me all about it."

It did take a long time, because Shelby couldn't stop crying in between. And when she was through, Edie was muttering to herself.

"That horrible man," Edie grumbled.

"He's that," Shelby agreed tearfully. She dabbed at her eyes with a paper towel. "I never knew I could hate anybody so much!"

"Well, from now on, you let Danny come here, or you go to see him at the office, but don't go back to that ranch."

"I never will. I swear I *never* will," Shelby agreed miserably.

"Oh, how could he!" she groaned, and the tears started all over again.

The phone rang suddenly in the silence that followed, and Edie patted Shelby's shoulder as she went to answer it. "You just sit there, honey, I'll get it. It's probably just Andy wanting to know if he can come over tonight. We kind of had a date."

"I can go out...." Shelby offered quickly.

"No, you can't. We'll work it out. Just drink your coffee, okay?" And she left her friend sitting at the table, looking lost and forlorn.

Edie was back in scant minutes, her face troubled. "It's for you, Shelby," she said. "Sounds like long distance."

Shelby sat erect with a jerk. "It's not King?"

"No. But it is a man," came the quiet reply.

Puzzled, Shelby went to the phone

and sank down on the sofa as she put the receiver to her ear. "Hello?" she asked tentatively.

"Shelby? It's Brad. Your stepfather, remember?" he added kindly. "I...I don't exactly know how to put this."

"Is it mother?" she asked quietly.

"Yes."

"Is it bad?" she persisted, feeling something heavy inside her.

"Yes."

"Tell me, then," she said gently. Her eyes darted to Edie, who was standing quietly in the doorway, watching.

Brad hesitated, and Shelby pictured him—a tall, graying man with an inherent dignity who found her mother beautiful but just a little too flighty at times.

"She took an overdose of sleeping pills," Brad said heavily.

"She...died ten minutes ago. Can you come?"

Shelby's fingers tightened on the receiver. Her mind whirled with memories. Her dark-eyed mother smiling in front of the cameras, a flash of black hair and olive skin, and dripping diamonds. Parties that never seemed to end with an ever-present glass in her mother's hand and angry glances directed toward the little girl who was always in the way. That last fight...

"Died?" Shelby repeated softly.

"Can you come, Shelby?" Brad repeated, his voice suddenly breaking. "I...we need to make some arrangements. There are reporters all over the place."

"Do you know why she did it?" Shelby asked huskily.

There was a harsh sigh on the other end of the line. "They canceled her contract. The studio said she was too old and too temperamental to stomach any longer. They'd offered her the role of a grandmother in some new film, and she threw a fit in the studio head's office. She forgot that the old days of the star system were long gone. They simply dropped her. She couldn't take that. She wouldn't even talk to me about it. The hurt went too deep.''

How like Maria Kane, Shelby thought miserably, to put her own interests first. Her beauty had been shallow like her personality. There'd been no strength in it, no steel to temper that delicate beauty. All of it had been surface. But in spite of that, she was Shelby's mother, and Shelby still cared.

''I'll be on the next plane. Are you at the house?'' she asked Brad.

''Yes.'' He cleared his throat. ''I'll meet you at the airport.''

''I'll be on the next flight out. I'll

call you from this end and let you know which flight I'll be on. Brad...thank you for calling.''

She placed the receiver down gently, and new tears replaced those she'd cried over King.

''Your mother?'' Edie asked.

She nodded. ''Suicide,'' she whispered, admitting it, hating the word, hating the implication of it. ''I'll have to go.''

Edie put a comforting arm around her. ''You poor kid,'' she murmured. ''All at once...Shelby, I'll come with you.''

But Shelby shook her head. ''This is something I have to do alone. I don't need anyone,'' she lied convincingly. ''Thank you, anyway, but I'll go by myself. And don't tell Danny,'' she added. ''He'd want to come, and just being connected with me right now could destroy his career. The reporters will have a field day. A scandal like this isn't the best publicity for an up and coming conservative young lawyer. Even his monied background wouldn't save him, and you know it.''

''Don't you ever think about yourself?'' Edie grumbled. ''Danny wouldn't mind.''

''That's why we're not going to tell him,'' she smiled. ''I'm right, Edie. You know I am.''

''Knowing it won't make Danny any happier.''

''He won't know until he reads it in the papers, and then it'll be too late. And when King reads about it, he'll stop Danny from going.'' She couldn't keep the bitterness out of her voice. ''He won't let his brother get mixed up in that kind of scandal. It might damage his merger with the Culhanes.''

''His what?''

''Never mind. I've got to get my

suitcase. How lucky," she added quietly, "that I hadn't unpacked."

Brad met her at the airport and took her to the palatial estate outside Hollywood, in the hills that overlooked the city. He carried her suitcase inside, leaving her alone in the blue and white decor of the living room, with its chrome furnishings. It was like her mother somehow. Stark and lifeless. She closed her eyes briefly.

"I've moved into town, into my old apartment," Brad said quietly. "I thought you might rather have the place to yourself, and there are two daily maids, Melissa and Gerrie—you saw them as we came in. Melissa's the little blonde, Gerrie's the brunette. They'll take care of you. Melissa's been doing the housekeeping, too, since Mrs. Plumer quit. She'll see you get meals while you're here." He perched himself on the edge of the sofa. "There are things we need to talk about. Burial..."

"She had a plot," Shelby said idly, naming a local funeral home and cemetery. She picked up a picture of her mother, a flashy publicity shot in a gilded frame that showed her perfectly capped teeth.

"We set the funeral for day after tomorrow," Brad said. "Is it all right with you if we have her friends as pallbearers?" He named six of her mother's closest male friends from years past.

She nodded quietly. "I don't mind." She looked up into his pale eyes. "Brad, did...did she go easily?"

He smiled. "She never regained consciousness. She just went to sleep," he said, his voice fading away. He bit his thin upper lip and the shimmer of tears dampened his eyes. "Went to sleep. She looked so beautiful...." His voice broke. He took a deep breath and went to the bar to pour himself a drink. He offered Shelby one, but she refused.

She sat down in an armchair and stared blankly at the deep blue of the sofa across from it, so dramatic a color against the deep white shag carpet. The contrasts suited her mother.

All of a sudden, she felt a sense of terrible regret. Perhaps if she'd tried a little harder, the distance between the two of them might have been breached. But her mother hadn't even tried. Not at all.

"Did she leave a note, or anything?" she asked Brad.

He shrugged. "No note, no nothing." He glanced at her. "No money either, I'm afraid," he said apologetically. "You know how she liked to spend it. The house is all that's left, and its sale will barely clear the bills.''

''It doesn't matter,'' Shelby said kindly. ''I have a good job, you know, and very frugal tastes.''

He flushed and looked uncomfortable. ''I wasn't implying...''

''I know you better than that,'' she reminded him. ''She stayed with you a long time. I think she really cared, Brad.''

His eyes dropped to his glass. ''As much as she was capable of caring, yes, I think she did. I'm sorry you weren't included in those vagrant affections of hers. She didn't like being reminded that she had a grown daughter. You see,'' he added wistfully, ''she wasn't grown herself.''

Shelby nodded. ''I know.''

The house was terribly empty when Brad left. He and Shelby had gone to the funeral home earlier in the evening, and she came away feeling hollow, carrying with her the sight of her mother lying there like some beautiful marble sculpture on that lacy white background. The picture haunted her, and she almost asked Brad not to go. But he was just as torn up, and looked as if he needed more than anything a few hours at his favorite bar.

The maids went to their quarters shortly after Brad left, and Shelby sat there amid all the glamour and luxury of her mother's house, and wept for the childhood she never had.

The phone was lying carefully off the hook. That had been necessary, because as soon as she and Brad went to the funeral home, they were besieged by reporters. It was news to most of them that the infamous Maria Kane had a grown daughter, and they went after her in droves. Where did she live, what did she do, how did she feel about her mother's death? It was suicide, wasn't it? Did she know why her beautiful, famous mother had taken her own life?

It was an accident, Brad told them, losing his temper after they'd been hounded all the way out to the car. It was simply an overdose of sleeping pills, not suicide! But the press didn't buy it, and in spite of their attempts at evasion, a carload of eager journalists tracked them back to Maria's house.

Brad finally went out through the basement and escaped. But there were still two or three of the newsmen left outside the front door, one of them with a crew of cameramen and lights from a local television station. They'd finally given up banging on the door, but they were still calling to Shelby through it in the dark, faintly lit by the outside torchlights.

They were still waiting, like persistent vultures. Waiting.

She heard a noise outside, and, thinking it was the reporters again, she ignored it. There came a loud, hard banging on the door.

Her small hands went to her ears and she stood there in the middle of the living room and screamed. And screamed. And screamed, until the banging finally stopped. She collapsed onto the floor in a heap of beige with the silky caftan she'd found crumbling into soft folds around her slender young body as she shook with the force of the sobs she'd held back for so long. She'd never felt more alone and lost and hopeless. Her heart was breaking for what she'd never had—for love and affection and a little kindness.

Like a dam breaking in the dark, she let all the emotion flow out of her in a burst of tears. She heard footsteps and the sound of the maid's voice, along with a deep, quiet male voice that grew steadily nearer. Then there was the thud of a door closing, and Shelby felt eyes on her bent head.

She looked up into a face she'd never thought to see again, into eyes that were narrow and dark with compassion as they traced the pathetic little figure alone on that thick, spotless white carpet.

"What...are you doing here?" she asked in a choked, husky voice, seeing him blur as the tears misted in her eyes. Remembering what he'd said to her at their last meeting, her face closed up like a petal in darkness, her eyes big and wounded and hurting as they met his.

"I came to see about you," he said tightly.

He was wearing a dark suit, the ever-present cream Stetson clutched tight in one dark hand, his boots gleaming in the light of the chandelier. His face was lined and haggard, as if he needed sleep, and his jaw was taut.

Her lower lip trembled, but she lifted her face proudly. "I don't need anyone, thank you," she said in a strangled voice.

His jaw clenched. The hand that was holding his hat almost crushed the brim. "Oh, honey," he said softly.

A sob broke from her lips and her eyes winced with the pain. "I hurt, King!" she whimpered.

"I know." He threw the hat onto a chair and lifted her up into his hard arms, crushing her slender body against the length of his, and she felt the warm, awesome strength of him. Her arms went jerkily around his broad shoulders, clinging, her nails biting into the fine material of his dark suit coat.

"Hold me," she sobbed. "Hold me tight. Make it stop hurting…!"

"Time will do that." His lips brushed her soft throat. "Let it out, honey. Cry it all out. I'm not going anywhere." He rocked her like a baby, comforting, caring. "Cry it out, Shelby."

It took a long time, and she could hardly accept the irony of being comforted by her worst enemy. But maybe he felt a truce was in order in view of the circumstances. Finally, when she felt drained and numb, he mopped her face with his handkerchief and made her blow her red nose.

He found the little blonde maid and had her make a pot of coffee while Shelby went to wash her face and get herself back together. He was sitting comfortably on the sofa when she came back, with his long legs crossed in front of him and his jacket and tie off. He looked the picture of masculine elegance, dark and sensuous and vaguely threatening as his hard eyes traced her body in the silky caftan.

"That damned thing doesn't suit you," he said bluntly. "It's too frivolous."

She sat down in the big armchair, tucking it around her curled up legs. "It was my mother's," she said. "I forgot to pack a gown."

He lifted a glass full of amber liquid. "I helped myself," he said quietly. "It was a hell of a quick trip, and I haven't slept since night before last.

She gaped at him. "You flew here?"

"I flew."

"A commercial flight," she said softly.

He shook his head. "My Cessna."

"You could have crashed it with that little sleep!" she burst out, horrified as she thought of all the things that could have gone wrong and caught him unaware if his mind had been foggy.

He gave her a faint smile. "I don't think so." His eyes traced her flushed face. "Worried about me, Shelby?"

She averted his gaze to the suit coat he'd thrown carelessly beside him on the sofa. "I'd worry about anyone on a trip that long without sleep."

"Nicely parried." He downed the drink and set the empty glass on top of the coffee table. He lit a cigarette and pulled an ashtray within easy reach of his hand. "Where's your stepfather?"

"In the nearest bar, I imagine," she sighed. "He loved her very much."

His expression was moody, brooding, as he leaned back against the plush sofa cushions, smoking his cigarette while he watched her. "Yes," he said absently, his eyes narrow, "I imagine he did."

"Would you like something to eat?" she asked as the little blonde maid, Melissa, brought the coffee on a tray and left it for them on the coffee table.

He shook his head, dismissing the girl with a look that made Shelby's blood burn.

"I'm not hungry," he said, with a quick glance at Shelby that didn't miss the flareup in her eyes. "Are you?"

She shook her head quickly. "I don't feel very much like food."

He took the cup of coffee she poured for him and leaned back again. "Tell me about her, Shelby."

She drew her knees up and wrapped her arms around them, curling up in the big armchair. "I didn't know her very well," she admitted.

"My mother had very little time for me. My aunt actually raised me."

"Not a close relationship?"

"No," she said softly. "Not at all. I was constantly in her way when I was growing up. I used to think she accepted roles that meant she had to go on location to film just to get away from me." She smiled wistfully. "When she was home, the house was always full of people. The parties went on all night. I was in the way. Always in the way. Of course, there was usually a housekeeper to put me to bed." Her face went rigid, her eyes clouded, and she gripped the coffee cup.

"Men, Shelby?" he asked gently.

"A parade of them." She shivered, and her eyes closed. "Stepfathers, boyfriends... Brad lasted longer than most, but he was only one of many. I could never..."

"What happened?" he asked quietly.

She licked her dry lips. "She married a European film star when I was fourteen. He liked young girls...and she was jealous I suppose of any attention he gave me." Shelby's big, dark eyes met King. "And mother kicked me out." Her eyes fell away from the sudden fury in his. "I went to live with my aunt. Mother tried to buy my affections back when the marriage went on the rocks, but not because she cared. It was only a gesture. She...hated me from the day I was born."

He drew a deep breath. "My God, no wonder it upset you when I mentioned her," he said finally. He let the frosted glass dangle in his lean fingers. "You might have told me, Shelby."

"And given you another stick to beat me with?" she asked softly.

His jaw clenched. "I suppose it seemed that way, didn't it?"

"But you didn't really have anything to worry about," she reminded him. "I never planned to marry Danny. If you want to know the truth, I like him too much for that."

He scowled at her. "That's a strange way to put it, honey."

"I didn't get a very good impression of marriage," she sighed.

"It isn't always like that."

She smiled at him. "How would you know, Mr. Brannt?" she asked mischievously. "You've never been married."

His eyes darkened. "I came close. If she hadn't been such a damned little flirt...." He leaned over and crushed out his cigarette, only to light another one, and Shelby held her breath as he studied its fiery tip. "She was a lot like you, city lady," he said bitterly. "All looks. The first day I carried her around the ranch, she started turning green. When I mentioned children, she turned around and ran. My money didn't compensate for that one demand I'd planned to make on her.''

She leaned her chin on her drawn-up knees in the concealing folds of the caftan. ''Did you love her?''

One dark eyebrow went up. ''I wanted her.''

''There's a difference, they tell me,'' she observed.

''Don't you know, young Shelby?'' he mused.

Her eyes fell before he could read the vulnerability in them that he fostered. ''No,'' she lied. ''I wouldn't know. I...I don't have time to get involved with men. My life is too ordered.''

''And you like it that way, don't you, honey?'' he asked with keen perception. ''You don't like any kind of intimacy with a man, even verbal.''

She lifted her coffee cup from the table and sipped the lukewarm liquid. She didn't answer him.

Outside there was the sound of a car engine cranking up.

''Maybe they got sleepy,'' King remarked with a faint grin.

''The reporters, you mean?'' She shuddered involuntarily. ''I'm afraid to go out there tomorrow. It's frightening...all those microphones and cameras.''

''You, afraid of a camera?'' he taunted.

''Now, yes,'' she whispered, closing her eyes.

''I didn't mean it like that.'' He leaned forward, studying her. ''You must know how lovely you are, little girl.''

Her eyes opened and looked straight into his, surprising a look in his eyes that she couldn't begin to understand.

"They'll follow you home, Shelby," he said quietly. "Your mother was old news, but you're something new to pick to pieces. Until the scandal dies down, you're the best copy going."

Her slight chest lifted and fell. "I know."

He set his glass down on the table. "Come home with me, Shelby."

She looked up, shocked. "What?!"

"Come back to the ranch with me. It's the one place you'll be safe. I can protect you."

"Forgive me for asking," she said breathlessly, "but why would you want to? When I left last time..."

His eyes exploded in brown flames. "I could have taken a horsewhip to you and Danny both for that charade," he said tightly. "But that's past history. I won't cut you into fish bait until you've had time to heal. But you won't see any peace at all if you go back to that hole of an apartment you share with your girlfriend.''

"It's not a hole!" she protested. "And just because I'm not up to my ears in money!"

"Calm down. I wasn't trying to insult you.''

"Weren't you?" She sighed wearily. "King, it won't work. You'll be at my throat the minute we get to Skylance, and I don't want to fight anymore. I'm so tired…''

His eyes took in the paleness of her elfin face, the lines that grief and sleeplessness had added to it. He crushed out his cigarette and got up, moving lazily toward her chair. He reached down and lifted her gently in his hard arms.

"King!" she whispered shakily.

"Don't panic," he said quietly.

"You're safe enough." He carried her back to the sofa with him, and sat down, cradling her across his lap. "Just be still, Shelby. I won't hurt you."

Inch by inch, she relaxed against his warm, strong body, letting her cheek ease down on his shoulder, letting her eyes close as the fatigue began to take its toll.

He shifted, drawing her closer, his cheek resting on her soft hair in the sudden stillness of the big, empty room.

"Go to sleep, little girl," he said softly. "I'll keep the wolves at bay for you."

She snuggled closer. "You can be nice."

"When I have to," he agreed quietly. "I don't particularly like being nice to you."

"I know. Why, King? Do you really hate me that much?'' she asked drowsily.

He laughed bitterly. ''Remind me to tell you all about it someday. Close your eyes.''

She obeyed him and felt the world fading in and out as drowsiness washed over her like a warm, comforting wave. In seconds she was fast asleep in his arms.

She woke up feeling warm and safe, and snuggled against something padded that seemed to pulse under her ear. Her eyes opened slowly and she saw that the pillow was a silky white shirt with bronzed flesh peeking out of the opening down its front, along with a patch of curling dark hair. She blinked. Under her ear was a hard, heavy heartbeat.

She lifted her head and looked straight into King's faintly amused dark eyes, suddenly aware of the warm, masculine body pressed against the length of hers.

"I thought you didn't sleep with men," he murmured.

She flushed. "I...what happened?"

"I couldn't pry you loose," he said bluntly. He reached in his pocket for a cigarette and lit it, one lean arm still holding her at his side. He pulled an ashtray closer on the coffee table and settled back.

"I'm sorry," she murmured.

His hand pressed her closer to his side for an instant. "Don't apologize. I like the feel of you. It's been a long time since I've held a woman through the night."

"Oh," she gulped.

"Could you manage not to sound so damned outraged?" he growled. "My God, Shelby, I'm a man. I've never pretended to be a saint."

She flushed. "I didn't imagine that you were."

"Didn't you?" He turned his head sideways to study her through narrowed eyes. "I had the distinct impression not so long ago that you didn't think I'd know a woman from a heifer."

The blush deepened because, in her innocence, she'd honestly mistaken that cool exterior of his for an equally cool nature.

"That's just what I thought," he murmured.

Her eyes fell to the open collar of his shirt. "I wasn't sitting in judgment on you."

"But you thought that, all the same." He tilted her chin up so that he could see her eyes. "You found out just how hot-blooded I was the night we made love in my study. Was it a shock, Shelby?"

Her eyes dilated wildly, and her

mouth opened on a wave of embarrassment.

He moved, so that he was above her, leaning over her, with the cigarette smouldering in the hand he propped over the back of the sofa. His dark eyes burned down into hers.

"The maids…" she whispered.

"It'll be an education for them," he murmured, bending. His mouth caught hers roughly, hurting her. He drew back, eyes glittering, narrow. "Don't close your mouth like that," he said gruffly.

Her cold, nervous hands pressed against his broad chest in token protest. "King…" she whispered uncertainly, even as the throbbing excitement swept through her slender body.

"You know what I like," he said in a sensuous deep voice, "don't you, honey?"

Her breath came quickly, in erratic spurts, and she hated the magic he worked on her emotions. She reached up hesitantly and unbuttoned his shirt, fumbling a little because it was the first time, her heart shaking her with its wild pounding as she looked long and deep into his eyes. Her untutored hands moved under the open edges of the silky fabric onto the warm, hair-roughened muscles of his chest.

"Like...like this, King?" she whispered unsteadily.

He nodded. His forefinger traced the soft line of her mouth in a static silence. "Harder, little girl," he said quietly. "Make me feel it."

She blushed, but she obeyed him, liking the rough feel of the curling dark hair under her fingers, the solidness of the warm muscle.

He pressed one of her slender hands against the hard, heavy beat of his heart. "Feel what you do to me, Shelby," he said huskily. "This is what lovemaking is all about. Feeling. Sensation. It's nothing to be afraid of.''

"I know." Her eyes closed as his mouth brushed lightly against her eyelids.

"You're trembling." His body lifted for an instant while he got rid of the cigarette, then both his arms went under her, his hands at the back of her head, holding it steady under his dark, piercing gaze.

"Is it fear?" he asked in a rough voice. "Tell me!"

The urgency in his tone unsettled her, but the sensations she was feeling made it impossible for her to lie to him.

"No," she whispered achingly. Her fingers lifted to his face, touching it gently, exploring. "Oh, no, King, it isn't fear...." she whispered.

His chest rose and fell heavily, erratically. "Show me." His head bent, his lips parting just before they touched hers. "Show me, honey," he bit off against her soft, yielding mouth.

With a sob, she reached up and pressed her eager mouth against his, hungry for him, loving him. He answered that surge of passion with bruising urgency, as if all the control he possessed was suddenly and completely gone. She felt his teeth, his tongue, as he bent her to his will, his lean hands moving slowly, gently, on her soft, pliant young body. She stiffened instinctively for an instant and he drew back instantly, something in his dark, glittering eyes that she'd never seen before when he looked down into her flushed face.

"Do you want me to stop, Shelby?" he asked softly.

He was giving her a choice, and one she didn't want to make. Her eyes traced the lines of his face slowly, lovingly, as she realized with a start that she didn't want to get away. There might never be another time like this, and she knew she'd never love any other man so much. But before she could speak, could tell him, there came the sound of a door opening suddenly, and the soft, sweet intimacy between them was shattered.

Seven

Shelby sat up as King got to his feet and turned, just in time to see the little blonde maid entering the room. She barely heard the brief conversation about breakfast her mind was spinning so badly. She drew the caftan close around her, like a shield, and sat quietly on the sofa until the door closed again. She was trembling all over with reaction, hating the interruption even as she was grateful for it. He'd humbled her again, and she'd let him. Would she never learn?

"Shelby..." he began quietly.

She straightened her shoulders and got up, the reason for her presence in this house coming back to her with staggering force.

"The funeral..." she murmured. "I've got to call Brad and see when he wants us to meet him at the funeral home."

There was a long silence between them. She heard him sigh roughly. "I'll call him for you. Give me his number."

She nodded and went to get it from her purse. His voice was as curt and controlled as ever.

The funeral was a nightmare of flashing camera bulbs, questions fired from all sides by newsmen and gossip columnists, and sobbing from Maria's heartbroken public. Brad stayed on one side of Shelby, King on the other, all the way through the brief service in the funeral home chapel. It was filled to capacity, and television cameras were outside when the pallbearers carried the ornate coffin out to the hearse.

Just as Shelby was being put in the black limousine, a reporter bumped into King and jumped in front of him. "Excuse me, cowboy," he said insolently, and rammed a microphone under Shelby's surprised nose. "Honey, they said Maria was pronounced dead on arrival at Hollywood General Hospital from an overdose—a deliberate overdose. Any truth in that?"

Shelby stared at the newsman blankly, still stunned by the sudden question. Her cheeks paled under the strain of the funeral, the frightening crush of people.

As she watched, the reporter seemed to grow taller. King had him by the collar and literally tossed him away. He glared at the newsman as if he were some new disease. "Make one move toward her again," King said in a dangerous low tone, "and I'll have your job, sonny boy."

The reporter stared at the taller man indignantly and started to fire back a retort when a pad-carrying reporter behind him quickly punched him. "That's King Brannt, you idiot!" came a loudly delivered whisper. "If you want to be standing in the unemployment line tomorrow, just keep on!"

The man with the microphone flushed darkly and moved away with a murmured apology.

King got Shelby in the car and slammed the door behind him, his eyes narrow on her white face.

"I should have decked him," he

said under his breath. "Are you all right?"

She nodded gratefully. "We...we should have waited for Brad."

"He's not coming to the graveside service," King said quietly. He leaned back in the seat as the car pulled out into traffic, loosening his tie with an impatient hand. "God, I hate funerals. Especially funerals like this, with mobs of people having hysterics for the benefit of the cameras."

Shelby bit her lip to keep the tears at bay. Her red eyes went to the window, and she watched the city streets, the routine of people coming and going, blankly.

King reached over and tugged at a lock of her thick hair. "I didn't mean what you're thinking," he said gently. "I know you cared about your mother."

A sob escaped her, along with a few stray tears. "I wish she'd cared, just a little," she whispered. "I seem to have been alone all my life."

His jaw went taut, although she didn't see it. "Not now," he reminded her. "You're not alone any more, Shelby."

She felt his big hand clasp hers, and she linked her small fingers into his strong ones, feeling the rough coolness envelope them securely.

"Thank you," she whispered.

He squeezed her hand. "Where do you want to go afterwards? Want to grab a bite to eat or go straight to the airport?"

She looked up at him. "To the airport, please."

He nodded. "We'll call Brad from there and let him wind up the details. Is there anything else you need to do?"

"No. Brad and I went to her lawyer's office this morning," she reminded him. "A notice has to run in the paper, but the lawyer will take care of that, and the sale of the house.''

''You aren't going to keep it?'' he asked.

She shook her head. She hadn't told him that her mother had died practically penniless. It would be like making a plea for sympathy, and she didn't need any more of that. It was the last thing she wanted from King. Pity was a poor substitute for love.

''I'll take you riding when we get home,'' he said suddenly. ''You need to get your mind off it, and the sooner the better.''

''Why are you being so kind?'' she asked gently.

He shrugged, looked uncomfortable, and turned his eyes toward the window. ''You needed someone. I couldn't let Danny walk into this. He doesn't need a law practice, but he seems to think he can't live without it. Getting himself embroiled in a scandal wouldn't endear him to those stiff-necked town lawyers he's associated with.''

''I knew you'd stop him,'' she said with a quiet smile. ''I hoped you would. I knew what it would do to his career.''

''I stopped him, all right. But he wouldn't have stopped me,'' he added adamantly, pinning her with his narrow, dark eyes. ''I'd have walked straight through hell to get to you.''

She met that look levelly, and felt the breath sighing out of her body at the intensity of it. She couldn't look away. It was as if his eyes were magnets, drawing hers, holding them, and she trembled at the undisguised passion she read in them.

''I want you,'' he said forcefully.

She blushed furiously and looked

away. Her heart shuddered in her throat.

His fingers contracted around hers. ''Don't panic. I'm not going to wrestle you down in the floorboard and attack you.''

The gentle levity brought a wan smile to her face. ''I wish you wouldn't say things like that.''

''I know. That's why I do it.'' He brought her hand to his lips. ''We'll talk about it at the ranch. Feel better now?''

She nodded. The hearse pulled up in the small road ahead, and she recognized the sprawling, well-manicured cemetery where her mother's plot was located. The last hurdle, she thought ironically. Just this left to go through, and it would all be over. She could put it behind her and go on living. With resolution, her hand went to the door handle.

* * *

The elder Brannts welcomed her back with mingled joy and sympathy and immediately set out to involve her in the ranch. Although she tried not to make it obvious, Shelby stayed out of King's way as much as possible. She found excuses to go places with Kate, to spend time with the two elder Brannts in the evenings when King was working in the study. Danny called every night to talk to her, and she felt guilty about the length of time she kept him on the phone, but it was another way of keeping out of King's sight since she could stay in her room when she finished the conversation. She refused invitations to sit with King while he worked. She refused invitations to go riding with him. And day by day his temper grew quicker and hotter.

She knew he was angry, but she couldn't help it. He wanted her. He'd told her so, and what King Brannt wanted, he got. She knew she could never say no to him if he asked, because she loved him too much. The only alternative was to keep him from asking, and she worked at it feverishly. By the end of the week she'd managed not to spend one single minute alone with him.

But Friday night upset all her plans. Jim and Kate announced that they were going out for the evening. Danny, who'd planned to come home for the weekend, called to say that Mary Kate was meeting him in San Antonio to take in a concert and he wouldn't be heading home until Saturday. And there Shelby sat, in the living room with King, who seemed to find more than enough to keep him at home.

"Scared, Shelby?" he taunted when the elder Brannts had gone out the door.

She swallowed hard. "Yes," she admitted in a bare whisper.

His heavy brows shot together. "Why?"

Her face lifted bravely. "You know what you said."

"Said? What did I say?" he demanded angrily. He thought for a moment and the scowl left his face. "That I wanted you?" he asked incredulously, his eyebrows lifting at her scarlet blush. He laughed shortly. "My God, what did you think I meant to do, drag you behind my desk some evening while I worked on the books?"

She gasped. "King!"

"Well, was it?" He slammed his half empty glass down on the desk, sending a drop of whiskey onto the glossy finish. "Damn it, you make me so mad I can't even think straight! Do you think I could enjoy making love to you if I had to fight at the same time?''

Her cheeks went scarlet.

''Or is that what you're afraid of?'' he asked narrowly. ''That you wouldn't be able to fight me?''

She lowered her face, unable to deny it, her hands clutching each other numbly in her lap.

''Well, I'll be damned,'' he said softly.

She heard him move, and the long, powerful legs came into view just in front of her.

He reached down and pulled her to her feet, holding her lightly by the waist. ''Don't you know how dangerous it is to make that kind of admission to me?'' he asked in a strange, deep tone.

She lifted her face, her big, dark eyes vulnerable as they met his searching gaze.

His hands tightened on her small

waist. He bent suddenly and brushed his parted lips against hers. She moved closer, her eyes half-closed looking straight into his as she went on tiptoe to return the strangely arousing kiss.

She felt his chest rise and fall erratically under her fingers. His hands contracted, hurting her, and she moaned.

He pushed her away and turned back to the small desk where his drink was sitting. "We'd better get out of here," he said tightly. "Go put on something pretty and I'll take you to that new little restaurant downtown."

"All right," she said, breathless. She almost ran out of the room.

Despite Branntville's population, it was one of the most expensive restaurants Shelby had ever been in, with white linen tablecloths and a frighteningly expensive wine list.

King looked vaguely amused at her puzzled expression.

"Didn't you think we had classy restaurants, little girl?" he teased, eyeing her over the wine list.

She smiled shyly. "I didn't think about it at all, really," she replied. He returned the smile, and this time there was no mockery in it. Her heart went wild in her chest.

"What kind of wine do you like?" he asked softly.

"Anything," she murmured.

"No preference?" His eyes narrowed. "I'm not trying to get you drunk, Shelby."

"I never thought you were," she protested. Her big eyes pleaded with him. "King, can't we just enjoy the meal..."

His face relaxed. "Relax, honey," he said, reaching for a cigarette. "I'm on edge tonight. I didn't mean to start on you."

On edge? She couldn't picture King that way, and he seemed to read the disbelief on her face. He smiled.

"I'm human, honey," he said quietly. "I get on edge just like anybody else when I've got something on my mind."

"Can I help?" she asked without thinking.

"I don't really think you'd want to provide the kind of help I need right now," he mused, and chuckled softly at the color that flamed in her cheeks. "How perceptive of you, Miss Kane, to guess exactly what I had in mind."

"Oh, hush!" she said, embarrassed.

"You delightful little brat," he said indulgently.

"I'm not a..." she protested softly.

"No," he agreed, "you aren't." His eyes traveled over her pale blue dress, lingering where it plunged in a V-neck. "You're all woman, and my blood pressure jumps every time I look at you.''

She caught her breath. "King," she whispered protestingly, looking around uncomfortably as if eyes were watching them. No one was.

"Look at me," he said.

She met his searching gaze, and felt her pulse throbbing.

"What were you going to tell me that morning at your mother's, just before the maid interrupted us?" he asked deeply.

She looked down at the white tablecloth in the soft light of a red enclosed candle in the center of the table.

"Or were you going to say anything?" he persisted quietly. "We didn't need words, did we?"

"No," she whispered unsteadily. "We didn't."

He caught her hand across the table and his fingers caressed it lightly as he held her eyes. "When we get home," he said in a deep whisper, "I'll carry you into the living room and close the door. We'll start over."

Her heart threatened to beat her to death at just the thought of it. Unconsciously her eyes dropped to his hard, chiseled mouth, and she remembered the rough feel of it against her own.

The arrival of the waiter interrupted her before she could stammer a reply. She concentrated on her food as much as possible, but when they left the restaurant, she couldn't even remember what she'd eaten.

King was quiet all the way back to the ranch, letting the sultry music from the radio fill the silence between them. It wasn't until they were on the porch that he finally spoke.

"I'd better tell you right now," he said quietly, "that I'm not playing games. If I take you into that room with me, it's very likely going to start fires that I can only put out one way. Do you understand me?''

Her lips trembled apart. She looked up at him with unconscious appeal in her dark eyes.

He nodded, as if he understood her even without words. His forefinger traced the soft line of her mouth and he smiled ironically.

"A month ago," he murmured, "even a week ago, I wouldn't have hesitated to take anything I could get from you. And now, when I know what I could get, I don't have the heart to take it. My God, honey, what are you doing to me?''

She only stared at him, her wide eyes sketching his face like a beloved canvas.

He sighed heavily and pulled her gently against him. He smelled of oriental cologne, an expensive scent that suited him, and tobacco. "You'd better kiss me goodnight and go to bed,'' he said in a half-amused, half-exasperated tone. ''I'm not at all sure I like these little webs you're weaving around me.''

''I don't understand,'' she murmured dizzily, wondering if this was really happening, or if it was just the wine going to her head.

''That makes two of us.''

He drew her up on her tiptoes and parted her soft lips expertly with his, his hard arms going around her to hold her gently against him. It was a strange kind of kiss, searching and hungry and exploring all at once. There was nothing of passion in it this time. He bruised her mouth as if it held all the treasure in the world for him.

His mouth skimmed along her cheek to the soft lobe of her ear, and his teeth nipped it lightly, sending chills down her arms.

Her arms clung to him when he moved away, and he disengaged them gently but firmly, holding her hands together against his chest as he studied her in the soft porch light.

"Bed, Shelby," he said gently. "I'm getting too old for platonic relationships."

She smiled at him, her eyes twinkling. "Are you old?"

He looked down his straight nose at her. "I feel about sixteen right now," he murmured solemnly. "But I'm thirty-two, Shelby."

"I know."

He kissed the tip of her nose. "Goodnight, baby."

"King..." she said softly.

He shook his head and tugged gently at a strand of her silky hair. "Go on."

She smiled before she turned and went into the house. It was the longest walk to her room that she ever remembered making.

Shelby went downstairs the next morning with excitement sparkling from her dark eyes, dressed in a neat pair of tailored jeans and a white tank top that set off her darkness. She felt a wild kind of anticipation as she went down the hall toward the dining room, as eager to see King as she was dreading it. What if last night had been a dream, and the reality was going to be that cold darkness in his eyes again?

She opened the door and went into the elegant dining room and found King at the head of the table. But not alone. A long-haired brunette turned her head and gave Shelby a cool, venomous look from watery blue eyes.

"Well, now, who's this?" the woman asked with a mocking little smile. "Danny's latest?"

"Shelby Kane," King introduced her, leaning back in his chair to spear a lightning appraisal down her slender figure. "Shelby, this is Janice Edson."

"King's latest," the woman added with an adoring glance at King. "I've been out of town or I'd have come over to meet you sooner than this, Shelby. How long are you going to be visiting us?"

It was like having all her dreams go nightmarish, but she didn't let any of the emotions she was feeling show on her elfin face.

"Just a little while," she replied, still standing beside the door. She wasn't going one more step into that room, not now.

"Shelby's mother died earlier this week," King said quietly. "She's staying with us a few days."

"Mother?" Janice stared at her for several seconds. "Kane? Maria Kane was your mother, wasn't she? Well, well, a movie star's daughter in our midst! I read all the Hollywood gossip columns, you know, it's a hobby of mine. I enjoy movies. Do you?''

Shelby swallowed uneasily. The woman was years older than she was, and cat-like in her cruelty. She couldn't stay and be torn to pieces by those red-painted claws.

She didn't know that she looked suddenly like a hunted fawn, but King saw that expression on her flushed young face, and something violent flashed in his eyes.

''I'm taking Shelby out for a ride this morning,'' he said, rising from the table. ''Too bad you didn't call before you came, baby,'' he told Janice. ''I'll be tied up all morning.''

''But I just got home...'' she pouted prettily.

''Come over for supper,'' he said, making the invitation with a carelessness that was lost on the older woman.

Janice brightened all of a sudden. "I'd love to!"

"About six," he added.

"I'll be here!" she replied with a vicious glance in Shelby's direction.

King took Shelby by the arm and marched her out the door onto the porch, closing the door behind them.

"I'm...I'm not dressed for riding," she stammered.

He tilted her chin up to his eyes. "Don't go cold on me," he said softly.

The smile melted on her, eased the hurt. "I...I could go alone," she offered softly. "You don't have to feel obliged to entertain me."

"I'm not sure exactly what I do feel, Shelby," he said solemnly. "But it damned sure isn't obligation. Come on."

*   *   *

"Can you really spare the time?" she asked as they rode out across the wide, gently rolling fields on a dirt trail made by years of horseback riding.

He smiled musingly. "No." He glanced at her from under the brim of his Stetson. "Any more questions?"

A lot, and all about Janice, but she didn't ask them. She turned her attention to the red-coated Santa Gertrudis grazing peacefully in the pastures that seemed to stretch to the sky.

"Jealous, Shelby?" he asked suddenly, reining in long enough to light a cigarette.

She schooled her emotions, keeping them on a short rope. "Of you?" she asked quietly. "I don't have any claims on your time, King."

His jaw tautened. "What kind of answer is that?"

She glanced at him through her

lashes. "The only kind you're going to get."

He smiled in spite of himself. "You little imp," he murmured. "Remind me to beat you."

"Not yet," she protested. "You haven't shown me the rest of the ranch."

He let the cigarette spiral its smoke into the air, his eyes brooding as they studied her. "Are you really interested in it?"

The question startled her, but she answered it honestly. "Yes, I am."

"That night...you were looking at a book on Western history," he said absently.

"I grew up loving it," she told him. "I used to read every Western novel I could lay my hands on, especially when I had to go back to Georgia. I took my modeling courses in San Antonio because there was so much history there—the Alamo and all.''

''And ranching?'' he asked.

''I cut my teeth reading about Uncle John Chisum and the Jinglebob spread,'' she grinned. ''Did you know that Branntville is located right in the middle of the Chisolm trail?'' she began excitedly.

He took a vicious drag from his cigarette and threw the remains down into the dust. ''Hell, let's get going,'' he muttered, suddenly irritable and impatient. ''I've got a lot of bookwork to do when we finish the grand tour.''

She followed along curiously, her eyes watchful on his quiet profile as he showed her his purebred stock and the immaculate, air-conditioned quarters where they were kept. He was proud of his accomplishments on the ranch, and he pointed out improvements in feeding and breeding as they rode.

"Let's rest a bit," he said finally, as they neared the river. "The sun's getting too high for riding."

She followed him to the shade of several towering oaks at the water's edge, dismounted, and sat down beside him. She put aside the ill-fitting straw hat he'd grabbed out of the tackroom for her.

"It doesn't fit," she murmured.

"Don't tell me your troubles," he said pleasantly. "You know better than to try riding without a hat around me."

"I've never had sunstroke," she reminded him.

"And I've seen too many cases of it not to believe in prevention." He leaned back against the tree, his long legs crossed in front of him, his hat pulled low over his eyes. He glanced at her. "You invite disaster, do you know it? You little daredevil."

She looked down at the faded denims on his powerful legs. "A little excitement never hurt anyone."

"Shooting the rapids in a canoe isn't my idea of a 'little' excitement," he observed. "Do you need that touch of danger to feel alive, Shelby? Does it substitute for what you could have with a man?"

She looked away. "I don't believe in self-analysis," she said softly.

"Maybe you should, honey." She was quiet for a long time, and he reached out and pinched her roughly. "Don't brood," he murmured when she jumped.

"I wasn't, really." Her eyes went to the river, gurgling as it ran over rocks on its way through the trees. "This river reminds me of the Chattahoochee River in Georgia. The name came from a Cherokee word that meant 'Flowering Rock.'"

"What was your aunt like—the one who raised you?" he asked suddenly.

She smiled. "Mean as a teased rattler," she told him. "She hated three things in life—men and pollution and her sister."

"Your mother?" he guessed.

She nodded. "Mother and Aunt Jane were as different as spring and autumn, in every way." Her hands toyed with a crispy brown leaf on the ground. "Jane loved the outdoors. She taught me how to garden and swim and even hunt. She could handle a 30.06 rifle with the best of them."

"Could you?" he asked curiously.

"I was afraid to try and shoot it," she admitted with a sheepish smile. "It had a kick like a mule and made a noise like the end of the world. I'm still a little afraid of guns.''

''I'll teach you to shoot a .22 rifle,'' he said. ''It's lighter and there's hardly any recoil. We'll go rabbit hunting this fall.''

''Shoot Thumper?'' she exclaimed.

He made a disgusted face. ''My God, that's a fairy tale.''

''No, it isn't,'' she protested. ''Poor little soft, fuzzy bunny....''

''Which tastes delicious,'' he said maliciously. ''Roasted, over an open campfire. Once you get a taste of soft, fuzzy bunny, you'll drool every time you look at one.''

''Cannibal!'' she accused.

He lifted the hat from his head and tossed it to one side. A lean, strong hand shot out and caught her wrist like a vice, pulling her down against his warm, strong body. His arm came up and pinned her to his chest.

"Now, what was that?" he asked pleasantly.

"Now, King..." she protested, laughing.

He tangled his hand in her straight, silky hair and jerked her head back against his shoulder. "Now, King, what?" he murmured, his eyes dropping to the soft curve of her mouth.

"I...I don't think you're a cannibal," she agreed.

"It's too late now, honey," he said. "We all have to pay for our transgressions."

Her breath sighed against his lips in short, erratic whispers as she watched the hard, masculine curve of his mouth coming closer to hers. Her hand touched his chest lightly through the thin cotton shirt, hesitantly, as if it were fire and she was afraid of a burn.

"I like for you to touch me," he

whispered roughly. "You don't have to go about it so cautiously."

"A man who likes to eat soft, fuzzy little bunny rabbits is capable of anything," she teased in a pale whisper.

"I'd rather taste you right now," he bit off against her mouth.

She relaxed in his hard embrace, letting his hungry mouth take what it wanted of hers. Her fingers traced patterns on the soft fabric of his shirt until he lazily unbuttoned it and led her hands to the damp warmth of the curling dark mat of hair.

He looked down at her hands against his body, and his eyes were dark and sensuous.

"God, you learn fast," he whispered huskily.

Her hands slid up and around his neck. She reached up and pressed her lips against his softly, warmly. "I like kissing you," she whispered, admitting it at last.

"I like it too, honey," he murmured against her parting lips. "Had enough?"

"No," she breathed.

"That's just as well," he whispered unsteadily, "because neither have I. Come here."

She felt the weight of him with a sense of wonder, her eyes open and staring up into the thick, dark patches of leaves on the oak tree as his lips explored her ears, her chin, the softness of her throat. If the world ended, it wouldn't matter now, she thought contentedly, because she had everything she wanted in her arms right now.

He looked down into yielded, brown eyes that openly worshipped him, and drew a hard, heavy breath. "Shelby," he whispered softly.

Her fingers traced the slow curve

of his mouth. "Thank you for letting me come here," she whispered. "Thank you for coming after me."

His lips brushed her fingers. "I'll never forget the way you looked that night," he said gently. "Why didn't you call me when it happened?"

"I...I wasn't on your list of favorite people," she recalled.

He sighed roughly. "No, you weren't. When I thought you were going to marry Danny..." His eyes met hers levelly. "But that wouldn't have stopped me from coming to help you, didn't you know that?"

She only shook her head, trying to make sense of what he was saying. "I was so glad to see you," she said.

"I noticed," he murmured. His eyes searched hers. "You slept in my arms."

A blush flamed on her face, but she didn't lower her eyes. "All night," she whispered.

He leaned down. "And I didn't want to sleep," he whispered back. His mouth found hers, cherishing it softly, slowly, exploring it with a thoroughness that drew a moan from her.

"King…" she whispered.

All of a sudden, he rolled away from her and sat up, reaching for his hat. "Get up, brat, and let's go."

She blinked. "Where?" she asked as he jerked her to her feet, barely giving her time to get her own hat on.

"To teach you how to shoot a gun."

"But I thought you had work to do."

He glanced at her wryly. "If we don't find something to keep us busy, little girl, you're going to wish I had work to do," he said bluntly.

She laughed, the sound of it echoing through the trees musically, and she thought she'd never been so happy. She felt like dancing, singing.

He caught her by the waist, reacting to that brightness in her roughly, his mouth grinding against hers for an instant before he lifted her into the saddle.

"I'll race you," she challenged.

"I'll beat you," he replied, swinging gracefully into the saddle. And he did.

The .22 rifle was easy to handle, and Shelby found she had a natural aptitude for it. She laughed when she hit the bulls-eye of the target King had set up for her in the woods just behind the ranch house.

"I did it!" she grinned, shaking her head in disbelief as she stared at the yellow center. "Annie Oakley, hang on to your laurels!"

"Don't get heady with success yet," he cautioned. "It was beginner's luck. You weren't even aiming properly.''

''I was so. I had it in the cross-hairs!''

''Like hell you did.''

''I did!'' she protested.

He came up behind her and reached around her on both sides, forcing her to hold the telescopic sight level with her eye.

''Like this,'' he murmured, close and warm and strong behind her. ''Aim down the barrel, see?''

''I see,'' she replied breathlessly. She wasn't as aware of the sight as she was of his lean, hard body, the warmth of it touching her all the way up and down. He smelled of cologne, and the feel of his rough cheek pressed against hers made her weak at the knees.

''Your mind isn't on what you're doing, Shelby,'' he whispered.

Her eyes closed. ''I know.''

"Neither is mine," he admitted in a soft, deep tone. "I want to turn you around and taste every sweet curve of your mouth. I want to feel you against me all the way up and down..." He tore away from her, his face hardening, his jaw like steel. He lit a cigarette, turning to scowl down on her young, flushed face intently. The only sounds were the cries of birds and the creaking sway of young pine trees around them.

"Can't you see what's happening, Shelby?" he asked tightly. "We're spending too damned much time together."

"I...didn't ask to come this time," she reminded him.

"Hell, I know that!" He took a long draw from the cigarette. "I'm going to send you home."

Eight

She heard the words through a haze, and at first they didn't register. Then, with startling clarity, they did.

"Send me...home?" she echoed weakly.

He sighed impatiently. "I want you until I can't sleep for thinking about it, is that clear enough?" he growled harshly. "I love my freedom, Shelby. I don't intend giving it up for a delicate little butterfly who'd have her wings torn off the first month she spent here.''

She let her eyes trace his hard face down to the open neck of his shirt. ''I haven't asked for anything,'' she whispered.

''You haven't,'' he agreed. ''But if you stay here another week, I'm going to. Every time I touch you...'' He took a deep breath. ''It's been amusing, Shelby. You were something to fill in the time with while Janice was away. But she's back now, and I don't need the diversion anymore,'' he added with deliberate cruelty.

She felt the world caving in on top of her. She could barely get the words past her lips. ''I...I'll leave in the morning,'' she said in a ghostly voice.

He nodded. ''I'll drive you to the station,'' he said quietly. ''Or the air-

port, if you'd prefer. I'll even buy
you a meal before you go.''

I'll buy you... It was the story of
her life. Her mother had tried so long
to buy her affection with expensive
presents. Now King was offering to
buy her broken heart.

She closed her eyes as she turned
away, feeling suddenly sick. ''You
don't have to bribe me,'' she whispered shakily.

''No,'' he said in a strange voice.
''I don't.''

She walked back toward the house,
leaving him alone in the dark forest,
watching, quietly, every step she took
until she was out of sight.

Janice was a knockout in an am-
ber-colored cocktail dress, and King
reacted to her as if she was the most
important thing in his life. He made
sure that she had place of honor beside him at the table, and, ignoring

the puzzled looks he was getting from his parents, he made up to the striking brunette all evening.

Shelby tried to ignore them later, in the living room, with Janice standing so close to King that she seemed a part of him, but it was impossible. She felt as if she were being stabbed, it hurt so.

Kate Brannt patted her hand comfortingly when King finally took Janice outside to look at the garden.

"I'm sorry you're leaving," Kate said gently, glancing toward the patio window where King and Janice had vanished. "King mentioned it, but when I asked why, he just stalked off without answering. Why, Shelby?"

"I came because King asked me here to recuperate," she admitted softly. "Now, he thinks I have and he...he asked me to leave."

"Oh," Kate said, taken aback.

Shelby sighed miserably. "Not that

I don't want to go,'' she said quickly.
''Getting back to work will do me
good.''

''But I thought your mother...?''
Kate exclaimed.

Shelby shook her head with a
smile. ''There was nothing left and,
in a way, I'm glad. She enjoyed her
wealth. It wasn't her responsibility to
provide for me all my life. I have to
earn my own way, as she earned
hers.''

''Oh, my dear,'' Kate murmured
gently.

''I think I'll go upstairs and pack,''
she said, rising. ''It's late and I don't
feel very well.''

''I know,'' Kate replied. ''You
have a very expressive face, Shelby.
I can almost feel the hurt for you. I
wish that my eldest son wasn't quite
so blind.''

''Janice is King's kind of
woman,'' she murmured. ''Poised

and sophisticated, and sure of herself. I'm none of those things. All I have is a face, and when it starts showing wrinkles, I won't have a career.'' She smiled wistfully. ''Sometimes I wish I'd been born ugly. At least then men wouldn't mistake me for a fashion plate without brains or emotions. I'm just a walking glossy photograph to King.''

''I'm sorry, Shelby,'' Kate said, and her pale blue eyes were gentle. ''I do wish things had worked out differently.''

''Is Danny coming home tonight?'' she asked suddenly.

''No, dear, he called late this afternoon to tell me that Mary Kate was spending the weekend in San Antonio with a girlfriend so that the two of them could spend tomorrow with some friends in the mountains.''

Her heart sank. She needed to talk to someone; but maybe Edie would be at the apartment. She nodded. "I still can't understand why he wanted to pretend we were engaged," she murmured. "He really cares for Mary Kate."

The older woman sighed. "It's a long story, my dear, and maybe I can tell you about it one day. Is King going to fly you home?"

"No!" she said quickly, flushing.

Kate nodded understandingly. "I'll drive you to town myself, Shelby, and put you on a plane. All right?"

"Thank you so much," Shelby said genuinely.

"I only wish you weren't going. You'll come again, soon?"

"Of course," she said politely, knowing even as she said it that she never would.

She went out into the hall just as King and Janice came back in. He drew the sleek brunette close by his side, and his face was liberally stained with pale pink lipstick. One eyebrow went up at the drawn look on Shelby's face.

"Turning in?" he asked coolly.

She nodded. "It...it's late, and I have to get an early start in the morning. I'm modeling in a fall showing of Jomar fashions."

"Jomar! How lovely," Janice cooed, "I do adore his designs."

"So do I," Shelby admitted, "although I only get to model them. I couldn't afford even a blouse with that label."

"You should have tried a little harder, honey," King said with a malicious smile. "You came closer than you knew."

"What?" Shelby asked softly, blinking at the sharp cut of his voice.

His eyes narrowed. "Your mother didn't leave you anything but a handful of debts, did she, Shelby? And you made damned sure I didn't know about it. Are you going to try and convince me that you didn't have a wedding ring in mind when you played up to me? God, I could have solved all your problems, couldn't I?''

Shelby's face went paper white. Where had he gotten such a ridiculous idea...her eyes turned toward Janice's face and caught the tail end of a triumphant smile.

''I read all about it in my latest issue of the Hollywood news,'' Janice said sweetly. ''Didn't you think it would come out about how poor your mother was when she killed herself?''

Ashen, Shelby turned and started wearily up the stairs.

''It was suicide, wasn't it?'' Janice persisted. ''How sad. I suppose it's some kind of inherent weakness. Hereditary, probably, too. Do you have suicidal tendencies, Shelby?''

"Let's have a drink," King said suddenly, drawing Janice toward the living room. "Let the little girl go to bed."

"Anything you say, sugar," Janice cooed.

Shelby went into her room and closed the door behind her.

King was still upstairs when she left the ranch the next morning in Kate Brannt's car, dry-eyed. This time the hurt had gone too deep for tears.

The days went by in a blur of activity as Shelby threw herself into her work with a vengeance. Edie tried tactfully to slow her down, but nothing would make her slacken the breakneck pace. Finally, in desperation, Edie appealed to Danny, who showed up early one Friday night as Shelby was getting ready to model at an evening fashion show.

"I'm sorry, Danny, I haven't time to talk," she said, feverishly sweeping the apartment in the sleek, sequined black dress she was to show, looking everywhere for the small matching purse. "I only have an hour."

"It won't take an hour," he said quietly. His eyes studied her closely. "You're going to fall down if you don't slow down," he said. "You're nothing but skin and bones."

"My diet..."

"Don't be funny, I'm not buying it." He jammed his hands in the pockets of his beige trousers. "He's really outdone himself this time."

"He, who?" she muttered as she searched under a sofa cushion and produced the missing bag.

"You know who. What did King say to you this time?"

"He said go home. And I did. End

of story." She smiled at him. "Want to come watch me work?"

He returned the smile, but without enthusiasm. "Just, go home?" he persisted.

"That's it. Don't third-degree me, okay?"

"He looks worse than you do," he said.

Her heart jumped, but she nerved herself not to care what King looked like.

"He works too hard," she replied.

"Both of you." Still watching her, he dropped down into an armchair and leaned forward, propping his forearms across his knees. "I tried to fly out to California when your mother died, did King ever tell you?"

She shook her head, making a big production of rearranging one small strand of hair at her ear in the hall mirror.

"He wouldn't let me come." He

laughed softly. "My God, I've never seen King move that fast in all my life. He'd cancelled two meetings, passed up a filly he'd have killed for at a foundation sale, had the plane serviced and was airborne less than fifteen minutes after he heard you'd gone to California for the funeral."

She turned, staring at him. "But...he hates me," she said unsteadily.

"Then hating you must do strange things to him," Danny told her, "because he hasn't been himself for the past six months. All anybody had to do was mention your name and he'd fly into a rage. He's been like that ever since your last visit, when you left walking in the middle of the night." He eyed her quietly. "You didn't know that he spent the better part of three hours looking for you all over the ranch that night, did you? Or that he rousted ten of the boys out of bed to help him? Or that, when he found out you were all right, he took a bottle of bourbon whiskey to bed with him and couldn't lift his head the next morning.''

Her face was pale when he finished, but she couldn't manage a single word.

''So mother and I figured that what was wrong with King was you,'' he continued. ''And we came up with the idea of pretending you were engaged to me, just to see what effect it would have.'' He shook his head. ''Boy,'' he said, ''what an effect it had!''

''He just didn't want you getting mixed up with somebody like me,'' she murmured. ''He told me so.''

''Bull,'' he grumbled. ''He couldn't stand the idea of your marrying me because he wanted you himself.''

"He's got a girlfriend," she replied, turning away.

"Janice, you mean?" he replied foxily. "How strange that he hasn't gone near her since the night you left."

"I don't care," she told him, her brown eyes wide and cool, despite her inner turmoil. "I never want to see King again as long as I live, Danny!"

He grinned. "You do love him!"

"Oh!" She turned away and opened the door. "I've really got to go, Danny. I have this show tonight, and another one at Jim Almond's in the morning," she added, naming one of the exclusive department stores downtown.

"All right. I'll be back. No hard feelings, Shelby?" he asked, serious now.

She smiled at him. "I like you very much. You can't really help it that you've got a rattlesnake for a brother.''

He chuckled. ''That's big of you,'' he said.

She sighed. ''It truly is. See you.''

All the rest of the night, her mind was on what Danny had told her. It would have been so wonderful if he'd been right—if King had cared. But she knew all too well that he didn't. He wanted her, which was something entirely different. And he didn't want her around him even though she attracted him physically. She really believed that he did hate her. And the ache was as potent as an open wound with salt in it.

The Jomar showing at Jim Almond's was exciting. He was one of Shelby's favorite designers, and she had an affection for the wiry little New Yorker.

She enjoyed the fit of the clothes

so well that she paid more attention to the announcer's description of what she was wearing than she did to the music or the people in the audience as she went down the aisle.

"...and it's the Western look this fall," the announcer was cooing, "with mix and match skirts and blouses. Here's Shelby in a two-piece casual suede suit, featuring a split skirt highlighted by cowgirl boots and a tasseled vest with a cream colored silk blouse and brown and cream necktie. Isn't she the picture of Western vitality?" the graying female announcer continued.

Shelby moved down the runway, opening the vest, gesturing toward the leather boots as she paused at the first row of chairs...and almost tripped when she spotted the tall, quiet man on the aisle wearing an elegantly cut brown casual suit with real cowboy boots and a cream-colored Stetson in the chair beside him.

"King!" she whispered, freezing in front of him.

Nine

She stood like a doe in the hunter's sights, ready to spring away, her eyes wide and frightened as they met the dark determination in his.

"I want to talk to you," he said gruffly, leaning forward in the chair.

Her mouth opened, closed. I hate you, she wanted to tell him, but the words wouldn't come.

"Isn't she a dream?" the announcer's voice boomed out. "In that outfit, she looks ready for some rugged cowboy to swing her up and carry her off into the sunset, doesn't she?"

"Which isn't a hell of a bad idea," King said with narrowed eyes. He stood up, towering over her, and abruptly handed her his hat. "Here, hold this," he said.

She took it without thinking. He bent suddenly and swung her up in his hard arms, ignoring her surprised exclamation and looks from the audience. The announcer loved it, exclaiming as King carried her, struggling, out the door, "see what I mean?"

"King, you can't do this!" she protested as he carried her through the crowded streets, attracting attention like a magnet as he walked toward a nearby parking lot.

"I'm doing it," he replied coolly.

"Put me down!" she cried, twisting in his steely grasp. "People are staring at us, King!"

"Let them stare."

She hit his broad chest with her fist. "I hate you," she wept piteously. "I hate you!"

He blinked, and a shadow passed over his face, but he didn't relent. "I know that," he replied quietly.

"If you don't put me down, I'm going to scream," she threatened.

He didn't break stride, or look at her. "Go ahead."

She looked around at the amused faces and decided that screaming probably wouldn't accomplish anything except to make those grins wider. She held herself stiffly until he reached the car and swung her down beside it.

He unlocked the door and put her in the small black sports car, going quickly around to get in beside her. She handed him his Stetson jerkily as her eyes rested on a newspaper folded to the society page. A picture of her was in a prominent place with a blaring headline under it—Model to Wed Heir to Brannt Fortune—Shelby Kane Will Become Bride of King Brannt in September.

"Now you know why I'm here," King said gruffly.

She stared at the newspaper with eyes blurred by sudden tears. So Danny had gone this far playing Cupid—announcing an engagement that hadn't happened to see what effect that would have on his older brother. And now King was going to blame Shelby for it, and she didn't think she could bear his temper again.

With a sob, she jerked open the door and was out of the car before King could catch her. She ran blindly out of the parking lot toward the street, and stepped off the curb just in

time to be right in the path of a bar-
relling semi.

"Shelby!" She thought she'd never
heard that particular note in a human
voice before. It didn't even sound like
King. But when she felt the lean,
whipcord arms go around her, dragging her out of the path of the truck,
she knew who they belonged to.

He crushed her body against his,
and he was shaking like a leaf. King,
shaking!

"Oh, my God, another second...!"
he ground out at her ear. His arms
tightened painfully. "You damned little fool!"

She bit her lip on a sob and closed
her eyes. "Why did you pull me
back?" she whispered brokenly. "It
would have been better..."

"No!" he whispered huskily. "No,
don't ever say that! Not ever,
Shelby!" He drew back and looked
down at her wet face. His own was

ashen. He looked like a man who'd seen death face to face. His hand reached out to brush the hair away from her cheek. "I always manage to say the wrong thing to you," he said tightly. "Or do the wrong thing. I should have left well enough alone."

She chewed on her lower lip, brushing at a stray tear. "Why did you...but I know why, don't I?" she wept.

He drew in a short breath. "There's a café by the river," he said solemnly. "Let's have a cup of coffee before I take you back."

She let him lead her to the sidewalk café and seat her at a small round table within easy steps of the river that ran through San Antonio. It was like being out in the country in the middle of town, and somewhere nearby was the sound of Mexican music.

She sipped her coffee in silence, not daring to look up. It hurt all the way to her soul, having to be with King these precious last minutes before she lost him forever. And she still hadn't explained that she didn't put the wedding announcement in the paper. If he'd even believe her.

"Are you all right?" he asked tightly.

She nodded. "Just a little shaken," she admitted, darting a glance at him. "Have you seen Danny lately?"

"This morning," he replied. His lean fingers circled the coffee cup. "He told me where you were."

"Oh." She sipped the strong black coffee. "I...I didn't do it," she whispered. "I know you won't believe me, but I didn't do it, King."

He stared at her blankly, and she wondered if he'd even heard her. His eyes were almost black, and there were new lines carved into his hard face.

"What's wrong?" she asked gently.

His eyebrow jerked, but he wouldn't answer her. "Finish your coffee," he said coolly. "I've got to get home."

She dropped her eyes. "Why did you bother to come?" she whispered.

"God knows," he growled. "It was insanity."

"Danny meant well," she murmured.

"So he told me." He finished the coffee in a swallow. "I may break his neck yet."

"They can always print a retraction," she said softly, looking up into his dark eyes.

His jaw went taut. "So they can."

"Did...did Janice see it?" she asked hesitantly.

"How the hell should I know?" he asked hotly. "I haven't seen her for weeks."

"But...."

"But, what?" he growled.

"Nothing."

"Have you eaten anything this week?" he asked angrily, his dark eyes tracing the thin lines of her body.

"Models have to be slender," she muttered.

"Not skeletal," he argued. "My God, Shelby, you look like a walking corpse!"

Her full lower lip pouted. "What do you care?" she asked thinly. "How I live my life is none of your business!"

His jaw worked jerkily. "Yes, you've just given me proof of that," he replied huskily. "You'd jump in front of a damned truck to keep me out of it, wouldn't you, baby?"

She stared at him blankly. "What do you mean?"

"It's a little late for soul-searching." He stood up with the check. "Do you want anything else before we go?" he asked.

She shook her head. Her eyes followed him to the inside counter where he paid the bill. If only things had worked out differently, she thought with a wistful smile. Even if he hadn't loved her, what she felt for him would have made up for it. And after she'd given him a son...

A son. King would love that, having an heir for Skylance. A little boy with black hair and dark brown eyes, and she could give him all the love King didn't want.

He came striding back toward her, his step quick and sharp, impatient.

"Ready?" he asked curtly.

She nodded, rising. He took her hand to help her out of the chair and she trembled at just the touch of it.

He jerked her chin up, catching the helpless attraction that she couldn't hide as it glowed from her dark eyes.

He scowled at her. "You might have given it a chance, Shelby," he said quietly. "At least you don't find me repulsive. That's a start."

"I don't understand," she whispered. "Given what a chance, King?"

The scowl got worse. His eyes narrowed, glittering down at her. "I think it might help if you tell me why you bolted out of the car like that."

"Why, because of the story in the paper," she told him quietly. "Because I knew you thought I did it, and I was afraid I couldn't convince you that I didn't. You see, Danny..."

"You thought *what*?" he burst out.

She backed away from the dangerous look in his eyes. "That you'd blame me," she repeated, wide-eyed.

All the hard lines left his face suddenly, and he looked down at her with blank astonishment in the place of anger.

"My God, Shelby," he said

harshly, "you'd rather run under a truck than face my temper? My God!"

She couldn't understand the anguish in his deep voice. He turned away from her and rammed his hands in his pockets.

"I didn't realize how hard I'd been on you until now," he said in a strange, deep tone. "I didn't realize I affected you to that extent."

"It's all right," she said softly. "I...I can understand how you felt."

"No, you can't," he said with a mirthless laugh. "You can't imagine." He whirled on his heel and studied her quietly, his eyes unreadable. "I've left my mark on you, haven't I?" he asked with smooth self-contempt. "You look like a walking skeleton, your eyes are red, and where there once was a carefree girl, now there's a tired old woman. God, I'm good for you!" he growled harshly.

He turned and started toward the car. "Come on. I'm going to put you back where I found you before I get you killed trying to run from me."

She followed him like a sleep-walker, still puzzled about the way he was behaving. Something seemed to be eating him alive, but she didn't know what.

She sat beside him in a daze as he headed back toward the downtown area.

"No, don't take me back to the show," she asked softly. "I couldn't bear it. My apartment's on the next street to the right, if you don't mind going out of your way..."

"I don't mind."

She didn't say another word until he pulled into the one vacant parking space outside the apartment building where she lived. She sat there, not knowing what to say, or how to say it, knowing this was the last time she'd ever see him....

"We've already said it all," he told her with inhuman calm. "Goodbye, Shelby."

She nodded. Her eyes searched his in a breathtaking silence while she tried to memorize every line of his face. Tears blurred him in her vision; tears that were hot and painful and unmistakable.

He scowled suddenly. "Shelby...?" he whispered, reaching out to brush a tear from her cheek.

She caught his fingers and held them against the softness of her cheek involuntarily. She could hear her pride shattering around her as she searched his eyes one last time.

"Kiss me goodbye," she pleaded in a broken whisper. "Please!"

In slow motion, she felt his lean, strong hands cupping her face, watched his eyes widen with disbelief and darken with certainty.

He bent, touching his hard mouth to hers with a tenderness that brought the hot tears swimming in her eyes, a soft pressure that ached with promise.

"Not like that," she whispered at his lips.

His hands tightened on her face. "How do you want it, then?" he asked huskily.

"Like this, King," she replied, reaching up to lock her arms around his neck, to draw his mouth down in the sudden trembling silence of the car.

She eased over the console with her lips clinging tenderly to his and slid onto his lap, feeling his arms come around her with a sense of wonder.

"Sports cars weren't designed for this," he whispered unsteadily as her mouth brushed temptingly across his.

"Weren't they?" she asked dizzily,

giving in to a wild impulse to feather kisses all over his hard face. She pressed closer against him, glorying in the effect she seemed to have on him.

His hands tightened painfully at her back, bruising her against his hard chest. His teeth nipped at her lower lip.

"What the hell are you doing?" he growled huskily.

"It's called making love, I think," she murmured against his answering lips.

"You're starting something you may not be able to stop," he warned softly.

"Promises, promises..."

He took her mouth roughly, his arms swallowing her, crushing her, as the devouring kiss went on and on until she thought she'd never breathe again, or want to.

"If you feel like this," he whispered, his voice husky with emotion, "then why the hell won't you marry me?"

She froze in his arms, looking up at him incredulously. "Marry you?"

He drew a steadying breath and smoothed her silky hair. "Shelby, I put the announcement in the paper. It was my way of telling you I wanted you for keeps. When you ran, I thought it was because you couldn't bear the thought of marrying me. Then, when I realized what was wrong, it froze me in my tracks." He caressed her flushed face with lazy fingers. "If you were that afraid of me, I thought it would be better if we forgot the whole thing."

She looked into his eyes with her whole heart in hers. "I ran because I loved you so much," she admitted jerkily. "And I knew it was always going to be one-sided...."

He pressed a gentle finger across her trembling lips. "One-sided,

Shelby?'' he asked gently. ''Let me show you how one-sided it is with us.''

He drew her up against him and eased her mouth under his, cherishing it so tenderly that she couldn't stem the tears that fell like liquid pearls from her eyes.

''You see?'' he whispered softly. ''I love you until I ache all over with it. I want children with you. I want everything with you, Shelby, good times and bad. But not if you're going to spend all those years running from my temper.''

She smiled up at him. ''But now I know what to do about it, don't I?'' she whispered, drawing his head down to hers.

''It'll take more than this sometimes,'' he murmured against her ardent mouth.

''Then you'll have to marry me and

teach me what else to do, won't you?'' she asked impishly.

''Be sure, Shelby,'' he said gently, and his dark eyes were serious. ''Forever is a hell of a long time.''

She nodded. ''Maybe it will be long enough,'' she murmured.

He wrapped her up in his hard arms and held her close against him. She buried her face in his warm throat and closed her eyes. Heaven could wait, she thought contentedly. This was paradise enough for one lifetime.

*   *   *   *   *

THE COLTONS

invite you to a thrilling holiday wedding in

A Colton Family Christmas

Meet the Oklahoma Coltons—a proud, passionate clan who will risk everything for love and honor. As the two Colton dynasties reunite this Christmas, new romances are sparked by a near-tragic event!

This 3-in-1 holiday collection includes:

"The Diplomat's Daughter" by Judy Christenberry

"Take No Prisoners" by Linda Turner

"Juliet of the Night" by Carolyn Zane

And be sure to watch for **SKY FULL OF PROMISE**
by Teresa Southwick this November from Silhouette Romance
(#1624), the next installment in the Colton family saga.

Silhouette®

Where love comes alive™

*Don't miss these
unforgettable romances…
available at your
favorite retail outlet.*

Visit Silhouette at www.eHarlequin.com

PSACFC

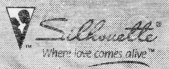

JAYNE ANN KRENTZ

Sizzling attraction, strong heroes and sparkling relationships
are hallmarks of *New York Times* bestselling author
Jayne Ann Krentz, writing as Stephanie James!

Here are two of her classic novels

THE CHALLONER BRIDE
&
WIZARD

available in one terrific package.

Don't worry—it's well

Worth the Risk

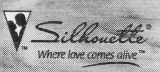